Death Wave 2012

By

Richard Sand

Award Winning author of the *Lucas Rook Mystery Series* and *The Immortal Dr. Fu Manchu*

A Lucas Rook Mystery

Copyright © 2013, Richard Sand

All rights reserved. No part of this book may be used or reproduced in any manner whatsoever without the written permission of the Publisher.

Printed in the United States of America.

For information address:

Fireside Publishing, Inc
10000 N. Central Exp., Suite 400
Dallas, Texas 75231

Library of Congress Cataloging-in-Publication Data

Richard Sand

Death Wave 2012

Library of Congress Control Number:

2012955529

p. cm.

ISBN: 978-1-935451-13-6

10 9 8 7 6 5 4 3 2 1

Fireside Publishing, Inc.
10000 N. Central Expressway, Suite 400
Dallas, Texas 75231

Also by Richard Sand

Fiction

Tunnel Runner
The Immortal Dr. Fu Manchu

The Lucas Rook Series
Private Justice
Hands of Vengeance
Watchman with a Hundred Eyes
Hell's Reunion
Blood Redeemed

Non-Fiction

Protocol – The Complete Handbook of Diplomatic, Official and Social Usage – 25th Anniversary Edition

Protocol – The Complete Handbook of Diplomatic, Official and Social Usage – 35th Anniversary Edition, Expanded

Girard College – A Living History

For my Big Brother, Stephe

With appreciation to my dear friend, Anita Cugini, for her hard work and support.

"Thus woe succeeds a woe, as wave a wave."

Robert Herrick

This book is a work of fiction. The characters, dialogue and incidents are products of the author's imagination. Any resemblance to actual persons or events is entirely coincidental.

CHAPTER ONE

Convicts hate anybody who hurts kids, maybe because they can't see their own. Or they hated themselves as kids, something like that. Whatever the reason, William Goodwin took more than a few beatings and a broom handle twice.

Then at last, there was the isolation. Isolation from the other inmates, the world and then, thankfully, himself. Time dragged, piled on him, and then on itself.

Like many prisoners, particularly those most harshly treated, and without hope, William Goodwin turned to religion. First, Orthodox Judaism, then Catholicism, forgiving but mystic, then Buddhism and Hinduism. By that time however, he was halfway insane, his mind broken the way his spirit and body had been.

The so-called professionals in the penitentiary were of little help to William Goodwin. There was a prison psychologist who wore thick black glasses, and seemed mostly interested in discussing the attacks on William.

The chaplain was no better. He offered no hope or forgiveness, but told the same story, over and over again, about St. Francis and Brother Leo, who were on a trip from Perugia, wherever that was. St. Francis kept saying that there was no perfect joy until you were beaten with a heavy stick so every bone was broken and then you were thrown out into the snow. This was where joy was found, said the chaplain. William wondered whether the chaplain wanted to hurt him with a broom handle like the others.

Then suddenly, the prison doors were open after a million days behind them. William Goodwin's freedom first meant nothing to him. He was outside the dimensions of his cell, but he felt he would fall off the earth. It was difficult to take a deep breath under the weight of his punishment and the guilt that he was the cause of his son's death.

No one came to meet him when he left his prison and went home. His wife was already gone. His daughter wouldn't talk to him.

There wasn't going to be joy or happiness or anything like that for William, but eventually there was some kind of relief when he began to believe he wasn't going to actually be beaten or raped any more.

"Try this, Billy," a psychiatrist told him after he was set free. So he took Xanax, the blue ones, four times a day and Klonopin, some times two of them at night and then Zoloft until he could at least realize that he was no longer locked-up.

"So maybe it was not you at all," another shrink said after a year or so. Not that it mattered, because by now William Goodwin's guilt had transformed itself into an obsession with the end of the World coming in 2012.

There was money enough from his late wife's insurance policy to help him look for a new life that might protect him from the Apocalypse. This eventually led him to The Tau, his new religion, and the group's home in Philadelphia. Then a lawyer approached him to file a product liability case against the companies that made the cold medicine that killed his son. The attorney would take the case for twenty-five percent because he was filing several other such claims.

But William Goodwin wanted somebody who would fight for him only. He'd seen Jake Schwarzman's pictures in an article in a magazine in the first lawyer's office, with a caption that said that he had once been a judge. So who would know better about right and wrong than him and who could better win a case than somebody who had decided them? Also the article said the lawyer's nickname was "The Swan", which William found out on the Internet were pure, loyal, and spiritual beings. These traits were going to be particularly important because of the coming Apocalypse on December 21, 2012.

William began to cry when he heard back from Attorney Jake Schwarzman that he was interested in a meeting. The retired judge sent a big black car for him and was very convincing about how the harm that was done, was to him and his son. A lawsuit would prove it was the pharmaceutical industry that was at fault. It would be in the papers and on television, if he wanted that, and they would all have to say how they were wrong and it was them who had been the ones who should go to jail.

William Goodwin knew that if it wasn't for his new lawyer and The Tau, which taught that the Last would be First, that he would not be able to make things right before The End of Days. But now he had found his new family and their religion and Judge Schwarzman after a long journey, and they accepted him. William Goodwin touched the wooden symbol that hung from the leather cord around his neck and took a deep breath. "*Ba-Abba*," he prayed quietly.

CHAPTER TWO

Former NYPD gold shield, Lucas Rook, looked at the watch he wore on his right hand to fool the bad guys. Just enough time to redecorate his one-room private detective agency, which meant losing the two pizza boxes, and depositing most of the mail into the circular file. Too bad the promo announcement of a twofer on dental implants wasn't a check from some fancy client.

A knock on the door. No need to slide the middle drawer open to reach your Glock since the latest owners of 166 Fifth Avenue had replaced the frosted glass on the office doors with plastic. It was the printer geek from down the hall.

"I've got your new business cards, Mr. Rook. You like the way I screened in the chess piece?"

"Absolutely," said Lucas. "Terrific."

"It's what we call, 'subliminal'. Much more subtle, yet effective. Don't you think?"

"Subliminal, absolutely."

The geek stood there, which meant he was waiting for a check. "There's our invoice in the envelope, Mr. Rook."

"Gotch ya, Louis. Paying bills the end of the week."

"Okay, then, Mr. Rook."

"Okay, Louis. Subliminal. Just what I was looking for."

Rook put the box of business cards and the envelope in the bottom drawer of his desk and made a bunch of calls, asking lawyers for work. You don't get anything, there's PP, personal protection, for your neighbor, blind supermodel, Grace Savoy. Pays decent. Plus there's that other thing about her saving your life last year out on the patio by blowing away the scumbag after he put two in you. "I did it by sound," Grace said, which is not believable except you're still breathing.

Lucas changed into his sweats after coming-up with zero business and rode the freight elevator down to the basement, where he banged away on the heavy bag now that those bullet holes in his chest were just scar tissue. Five rounds of the Gerry Cooney left and the Phil Quigley right. Then it was upstairs to take a "patrolman's shower," which meant washing whatever you could at the sink.

You get all neat and clean and it's off to see retired judge, Jake Schwarzman, who has a potential client. The Swan's law office was something between swanky and regal, which means you're wearing your black leather jacket with the turtleneck and just of hint of your .45 showing to complete the ensemble.

Serena doesn't give you the cold shoulder when you walk over to her desk, but that's only because she's seen your act a dozen times before and is smart enough to keep coming up with different ways to tell you "no" without busting your stones.

"New perfume?" Rook asked. Really clever.

"The Judge is running a bit behind, Mr. Rook. Perhaps you would like a cup of coffee and there's the latest edition of *Skiing*."

"The first part is good. You join me?"

"If only we did not have that non-fraternization policy. Such a pity."

"How long is he going to be, dear?"

Lucas knew she hated to be called that. Her intercom flashed and she picked up the phone. "He'll see you now. If you'll follow me."

They went down the hall to the corner office on the left, Serena giving it a little extra in the walk department.

"Thanks for that, anyway," he told her.

"Certainly, Mr. Rook," she said.

The Swan looked elegant as ever. Silver hair, two thousand dollar suit, fancy gold glasses, and the lapel pin for his nickname. This time, he also had a big band-aid on his neck. Schwarzman got up from behind his desk that would not have fit in Rook's office, and they shook hands.

"Dermatologists, Lucas, you know how they are. You walk into their office, they're cutting something off." The Swan sat down and turned on the air purifier behind him. Then he took out a twenty-dollar cigar, but didn't light it.

"As I mentioned on the phone, I have a client I would like you to meet. You may bill me, whether you take the case or not."

"I'm all ears."

"Involuntary manslaughter, Lucas. From the children's cold medicine he gave his infant son."

"So he could party, I'm guessing, Judge. My smeller's telling me he's a fiend for the slot machines, something like that. Am I right?"

"Accurate," said Schwarzman. "My client served some unpleasant time for that. I'm looking at the products liability case, which also might have helped him beat his criminal charges if he had appropriate counsel. I'd like you to at least meet him and hear what he has to say."

Rook got up. "Let me think on it, Judge. A dead kid and all. I'll call you."

Schwarzman adjusted his French cuffs. "He'll be here in half-hour. I would appreciate your meeting with him. Have a cup of coffee across the street, come back."

"I owe you for what you did with the law suit about me taking those shots up on my roof. You settling the thing and getting me the apartment, and all. So I'll meet with your client on two conditions. You alright with that, counselor?"

"Go on."

"One, I say what's on my mind. Two, if what's on my mind after the meet, is what's on it now, we're done."

"Fair enough," said The Swan. "One way or the other."

The spot across the street sold six-dollar lattes' with little doilies, so Lucas walked around the block and then east for two. There was a shoeshine stand at the corner with an empty chair, but you don't do that to Jimbo Turner, who's been your shineman since you and your brother walked the beat.

Lucas Rook had two cups and a decent cheese danish at Foxes. He left a buck for the waitress, taking the *Daily News* with him and was crossing the street to head back to The Swan's office, when Ugly Meg called out to him. Her face was pretty well busted up, which must have been for the four hundredth time.

"You don't say hello or nothing?" said Ugly Meg.

"Looks like some things haven't changed," he told her.

She shrugged her shoulders. "Get what I deserve, I guess," she said.

Lucas Rook went back to the lawyer's office. When he got there, Serena sent him right in to see The Swan, which meant the creep would be there.

Judge Schwarzman got up from behind his desk. "This is Mr. William Goodwin," he said.

Goodwin stood up and offered his hand. He was small and thin and still had that gray on him that you only get in prison.

Rook ignored him and sat down.

"My client has retained me to pursue his civil remedies," said Schwarzman. "He was incarcerated for four years and nine months."

"Danemora, I'm guessing," said Lucas. "How'd you do there? Not so easy for baby killers, I'm betting."

"For something which was not my fault," said Goodwin as he touched the small wooden cross he was wearing. "This must be made right. The Apocalypse is coming. It is."

"William," the Judge said. "I told you 2012 is only a year on the calendar. Everything will be fine just as it was with Y2K. No planets are going to crash into us. The world is not going to end"

Goodwin mumbled a prayer.

"There are significant issues," said the retired judge. "The issue of causation, forseeability, the labeling."

William Goodwin started to speak again, then stopped and raised his hand.

Rook turned to the ex-con. "Knock yourself out. But you bullshitting me is not going to get you anywhere."

"I used to work for the post office," said Goodwin. "Letter carrier, so I had the day shift. My wife, Maureen, worked at night. We had a daughter. She teaches school in Bayonne, but won't have anything to do with me. Maureen, she got terminal pancreatic cancer after our son was born. Our daughter helped until…" Goodwin looked up again, but at his lawyer, not Rook. "Maureen had a life insurance policy. And I'm going to spend it to clear my name before it's too late. Before the Apocalypse comes."

"Mr. Goodwin has recently joined a religious community and lives in Philadelphia now," the retired judge said.

Lucas got up. "Counselor, he said. "I'm going to 'mull' things over I think they say."

"I appreciate that," said The Swan.

"Me, too," said Goodwin. He offered his hand, which Rook refused.

"Can I call you, Billy?" said Lucas.

"Sure you can. Billy's fine."

"You had me going there for a minute," Rook said. "No, maybe a second, Billy boy. You kind of did. You know, you don't look like an evil, baby-killing type. You blend in like you're part of everyday life, right? Then you had to go and say 'Billy's' okay. Not Bill, Will, William. Billy's a kid's name. Halfway a little boy's name itself."

Rook took a half step forward and William Goodwin, two steps back.

"And the way that Billy-boy rat face of yours looked. You hated that kid. The crying, plus he cramped your style. You hated your own kid and you loved that casino, the flashing lights, and the girls in hot pants. They comping you 7 & 7's while your kid's dying? How'd that go for you?"

"Will you think about it overnight and call me tomorrow?" said Schwarzman.

Rook took a deep breath and then looked out the window and back. "I'll do that," he said and left without his usual attempt at Serena.

The Swan was doing what rich lawyers do. You're getting a hundred thousand dollar fee and maybe a civil suit after. Maybe that changes the baby killer into Mother Teresa. But this detective wouldn't do anything except hose the puke down the sewer.

CHAPTER THREE

There was a decent bar six blocks around the corner from Rook's office that meant no yuppies and beers that weren't seven bucks a draft.

Lucas was halfway to lit when he left, which made going to the office halfway a waste of time. But when you don't have any cases working, you got to try again to see what you could come up with, which is not going to include a job in the baby killer department. A couple more lawyer calls, maybe you get lucky.

The usual group of smokers was out front of 166 Fifth Avenue, including the printer geek, who gave you the look that he still hasn't been paid, even though you just told him it's the end of the week, which meant the end of the month anyhow.

Manny's kid was in the lobby changing the directory. "New tenants," he said. "Women lawyers. Double trouble, I guess you would say, Mr. Rook."

"Correct. An accurate call."

"And there was a weirdo-looking little guy, asking for you, Mr. Rook. I told him you weren't here and asked if he wanted to wait. He said he'd be back and it was okay because you knew him."

"Appreciate it," Lucas said. "Weirdo's about right. He comes back and I'm not here…"

"I'll take the bat to him like pop would have done."

Rook nodded and went upstairs. The phone was ringing when he got to his office. Lucas missed the last ring, but called Owls Miksis back.

"How'd you know it was me? I didn't leave a message."

"Caller ID, Owls. It's a regular thing now."

"Just got rid of my rotary phone, I did. Seven dollars a month for what? Highway robbers are what they are."

Rook popped open a Yuengling. "You called me, Owlsie."

"Right, right. Got something for you. Good all around. Not any domestic case, which I know you hate. It's compo, complete with fraud and a sleazy liar, I mean lawyer. Also to complete the trifecta, the client's a friend of yours."

Rook drank three cold swallows of the beer.

"You ready for this?" Owls said. "You must be, sounds like a brew you're drinking. Hope it's domestic."

"Domestic, it is, Detective Miksis. What do you got?"

"The 'what I got' is that the employer's self-insured, so I get carriers' rates with a little kicker. The 'who's' old Pinto Face, Phil Pizzolo. You interested?"

"All the way around, my friend. The usual arrangements, Owlsie?"

"The usual, except you bring me a couple of six packs of whatever you're drinking to seal the deal. Be out here by five."

"Cutting it close," Lucas told him.

"Pizzolo wants a meet yesterday. He's all squirrelly about this because he's riding bareback, no insurance and all. I told him I'd see what I can do, which means you need the file."

"Pinto Face knows it's me going to be handling this, Owls?"

"He does. That's half the fun. Come on out. I'm not here, I'm down at The Swede's. Tonight's pot roast night."

Lucas called over to Sid Rosen's that he was going to the Bronx and so have his vehicle out front. Sid talked him into taking the Avanti since it wasn't a long run and reminded him that the dealer from York was still asking about the car that used to belong to Rook's dead, twin-brother before he got gunned down outside of The Sephora Club. Rosen also added the tidbits that Mark Twain, Edgar Allen Poe, and Linda Lovelace all lived in the Bronx.

Rook swung Kirk's black fiberglass coupe out of the garage and took 6th Avenue, which the out-of-towners call, Avenue of the Americas, to the delight of every taxi driver in the City. Then over 72nd to 7th Avenue and across the bridge.

He had done the trip before in thirty-five minutes or so with the mufflers making their baritone sound, but it was asshole-to-asshole traffic, and it was an hour before he got to Owl's place, a little row house with a steel door.

Miksis adjusted his thick glasses. "I thought you'd given up on me. Then I tell myself, 'self' I say, there's dollars in this, so no PI worth his salt, not to mention he was a gold shield for New York's finest, is going to let this go."

"Traffic was fucked, Owlsie."

"So's eating cold pot roast. The file's in there on the dining room table. It's thicker than my hemorrhoid. Your piece of the retainer's in it. The second check's my advance on your expenses."

"You're a prince, Owls. I always said that."

"And you're a motherfucker, who knows his way around the block, which by the way is where my dinner's getting cold. Give an old timer a ride will you?"

"Will do," said Rook.

Lucas Rook reviewed the case in the car after dropping Owlsie off and then went down to Sheepshead Bay to meet Pinto Face. The meter was running since you're billing the client from the moment you get the file. Life wasn't all a bag of shit on an August afternoon.

Phil Pizzolo thought he was a big shot at the 1-5 where Rook first met him, even though all he was a sawed off prick, dressing fancy and getting the most out of his prematurely gray hair, which he said made him look distinguished. That was bullshit, but enough to get him this rich Jewish lady from Murray Hill, who took care of him until she followed Mr. Zeldin to the great wholesale poultry business in the sky. Pizzolo finished his illustrious career at the 6-1, where he opened his detective agency, which was really a guard business because he couldn't find some other old Jewish lady to take care of him.

The restaurants were starting to come back, in Sheepshead Bay. Lindy's opened again, and some clothing stores, so getting stabbed wasn't the problem like parking was.

Cops for some reason hate to get parking tickets, even though they could always get them taken care of.

Or if you're working some side job like now, you can lay off the expense. Partly, it's because the ticket says when and where you were, not that you're Son of Sam or whatever, but that's just not smart. And neither is flushing your money down the toilet, which is what paying the citations is.

You're going to get to the deli on Avenue U to meet Pinto Face early, because if you've ever done police work, that's the way you roll. Otherwise you're five minutes late and your wit is in the wind or the collar's been made and you lose out, or your partner's beat bad or worse. That and the parking, Lucas Rook's there at twenty of.

Some tree hugger pulls his hybrid out and Rook's got the space and sits there eyeballing Eugene's. Then Pizzolo comes strolling down the way like he owns the world, but still with the white patches on his face, vitaligo, he got the year before he put his papers in, which is why he's called "Pinto", like the bean.

Rook waited for Pinto Face to get comfortable in his booth. Then he went into the deli and sat down.

"Owls told me it was you," Pizzolo said.

"He was right."

The waitress came over with a cup of coffee. Good-looking blonde, but halfway like she's a weight lifter. She opens her mouth there's a Russian accent, which means she's probably got an uncle who sleeps in his leather coat and would stick you in an oil drum just because. They waited until Svetlana went to another booth before the conversation started up.

Pinto sipped his coffee. "Owls told you where this is, what I need?"

"Where you are, is half-way to being fucked. What you need is for you to have had compo insurance for your guard business, which I don't know why you're into anyway. The scummer file his claim yet?"

Pizzolo put his cup back down. "Skip squeezing my shoes, Rook. He got the lawyer who advertises on the buses, 'Cash' what's his name. It was some lawyer who wasn't a shitbird, if there is such a thing, I could make it go away myself."

Lucas let his coffee sit. "So he got his shyster attorney who sometime soon, if not already's, going to figure out you're riding bareback."

"Which gets me sued in a fall-down case for his so-called injuries. Worse, this maybe gets me turned in for not carrying insurance and maybe I'm looking at some state prosecutor opening a file."

"Owlsie gave me a copy of what you gave him." Lucas said. "Just what you would figure, the thing happens late on his shift with nobody around."

"The usual neck and back shit. The fucker's seeing some chiro in Jersey."

"You run an index on him?"

"Sure, sure I did, Rook. McGarvey's a regular pro. Two MVA's, another comp claim. Paperwork should be in the file. You can handle this, Rook, and I mean <u>handle</u> it, right?"

"Now, Phil, don't you worry about a thing." Lucas got up to go. "Except keeping current."

"Owls got the retainer," said Pizzolo. "I get the bill, it gets paid."

"Appreciate it, Phil," said Lucas. "I really do."

Rook drove back to his office, which you do only if you got a client paying your expenses, which are going to include not only travel at fifty-five cents per mile, but also the parking lot, which is going to be sky-high.

He popped open a cold brew and opened a file on Pinto, not only on the computer, but the old stand-by stack of index cards, which you could move around to get different looks at your job. Also you could throw the cards out. The computer, once you input something, it's there forever.

Lucas wrote up and billed an "initial evaluation" of the file and what Pizzolo had told him. You do it that way, you get to do a detailed evaluation after, and time is money.

What you've got is Fred McGarvey doing security work for the uninsured security company. You run your own claims index, which shows he likes having various types of paying accidents.

This time, it's two o'clock on a Sunday morning, He's got no criminal record, and so they're paying him $12.50 an hour. McGarvey's watching a truck full of electronic parts, he hears a noise, goes to check it out, and trips on a crack in the sidewalk. Probably not big enough to get him a personal injury case a decent lawyer's going to tell him, but with workers' comp, it doesn't matter. He finishes his shift, and doesn't do anything about it until Monday morning, which is when he sees his lawyer because that's when the letter of representation is dated to Pizzolo's company. Too bad there's no surveillance video.

Rook did some work on the Web that went into the billing. Then he took his car back to Sid's. Rosen was yelling at somebody on the phone, so Lucas pulled the Avanti in, chucked the garage man his keys and went back to his place in the St. Claire, which he still called his apartment, even though he owned it since The Swan had worked his magic on the shooting that happened up on the roof.

Bright and early the next day, you start a little spadework, which first, is you call a friend of yours at Allstate. Hobie Finnis was on the job for twenty-five before he took his pension and his understandable mistrust of humanity to the insurance biz.

Lucas got him on the first try. "You're not telling me I'm in 'good hands,' Detective Finnis. I thought you were supposed to do that."

"How's it hanging, Rook? Somebody I can do for you? You working on one of them fender-benders, our MIST program's a bear."

"Minor Impact, Soft Tissue. I think who I'm working already hit you up for one or more of those. Now he's running a compo scam that's got old Pinto Face's balls in the wringer."

"Phil Pizzolo, never liked him, not even a little bit. Last I heard he was tapping this old broad and she put him in business or something. Anyways, it's for you, not for him, so you let me go grab a smoke, and then you can go over what I got on the mope's auto file."

Twenty minutes later, Hobie's fax on the MVA comes in. Same shyster for the earlier auto claim, same chiro. He uses an orthopedist and neurologist who share the same address. Dollars to squad room donuts, the lawyer's got another set of specialists for the comp claim, so if you're asking for records, you're not getting the injuries from the MVA. This gives you another couple of hours of billing that is good enough that you reward yourself with a hot corned beef on rye you're going to inhale in front of the boob tube.

The new Ethiopian at the front desk of The Saint Claire had been replaced by somebody who got the same resentment under the surface. "A gentleman was here to see you, Mr. Rook. He said you have just met. He did not leave his name."

Lucas nodded and took his mail. No way would it have been Pinto Face, which meant it was Billy-boy again. He'd call Jake Schwarzman when he got upstairs and make it clear if he saw the child killer ever again, he was going to make him wish he were safe behind bars.

CHAPTER FOUR

Lucas Rook ate, and then stretched out on his sofa for an hour. After, he showered and changed his socks so he'd be all professional when he got the job going again.

Things were good because paying clients means you don't have to dip into that retirement from the PD. The meter is ticking, so it's off to do an eyeball. Maybe you catch the so-called, injured McGarvey caulking his windows or the like.

One time working a compo claim, you're following a scummer like McGarvey and you get stuck in traffic. All of a sudden, the guy throws one of those blue bubblegum lights up on the roof and starts hauling ass down the shoulder. There's a fire up ahead and the poor cripple jumps out of his vehicle, throws on his volunteer fire duds and starts running in like he's Jesse Owens. Bingo, there goes the job you're not looking to happen so fast.

Lucas Rook went over to Rosen's to get his vehicle out again.

"Going out to Queens," he said.

"Taking the IRT?" asked the garageman.

"I don't think so, Sidney. Running a case here."

Rosen wiped his hands on a rag. "I don't know. I like the sound of that, 'PI on the Subway'. Sounds like a perfect series for HBO. You taking the Avanti?"

"Somehow a fifty year old fiberglass sportscar's not so inconspicuous."

"Give me a minute, Lucas boy, and the Merc is yours."

"Appreciate that, Sidney."

"Okay," said Rosen. "You should know that Flushing is from the Dutch, *Vlissingen*, which means 'salt marshes.'"

"Of course, it does."

"And also, Lucas boy, you get the chance, visit Louis Lepke's grave at Flushing Cemetery, paying my respects to one of the toughest Jewish mobsters that ever was." He got the keys for two cars that were blocking Rook's vehicle. "You want me to ride along?"

"I'm doing surveillance on an insurance job that maybe I'm testifying about it later. So it's not a good idea for me maybe having to explain why you're there if something goes sideways. Then the puke's lawyer's finding a way to bring an invasion of privacy suit."

Rosen underhanded the keys to one vehicle and went to move the BMW in front of it.

"What's with all this 2012 nonsense, Sidney?"

"It's the end of the Mayan calendar, so there are lots who think it's the End of Days, of the World. Lots of crazy theories about meteors, the sun exploding, all that, but it's just another excuse for the weirdos to wring their hands, Lucas boy."

"Speaking of Queens," he said as Rook pulled out of the garage, "Two cops got blown–up by a bomb in the British Pavilion at the World's Fair of 1940."

Freddie McGarvey's place was a duplex, one of the new pieces of crap put up in Flushing. Phony bricks, wrought iron, and cheap siding. There was a picture window on the ground floor, not a very smart move unless you want some perp to join you for a late night snack.

McGarvey's was on the second floor with sliders out to a balcony just big enough for a portable barbeque and this old black dog, which was probably dreaming that there was actually grass and trees around. Three American flags out there, even though it was no holiday. You fly the flag and walk with a cane, people think you're a war hero, which Hobie's report says he had no service record.

Rook made two trips around the block, looking for a parking space, which is the most you can do without spooking somebody like McGarvey, who's been around the block himself. There were no spots he could eyeball the place from, so he parked up the street where there was a graveyard that Sidney was probably talking about.

Lucas went into the cemetery to make it look believable. No "Lepke" was buried there according to the lady in the office, but Louis Armstrong was in Section Nine and would he like to see that headstone. "A number of people do that you know," she said. "Collecting the final resting places of people of note is a hobby for many."

"Is that a fact," said Lucas. And he went back out to his car.

Freddy was taking his black dog out to take a dump, probably on the grass outside of the cemetery. The so-called injured security guard was walking with his cane, but no way was he using it for support. You used a cane yourself after the beating Etillio's gang gave you all those years ago, you can tell when somebody's showing it instead of using it.

McGarvey went up the block, Lucas eyeballing through his telephoto lens. The dog's collar said, "Sam". Then the sleaze is back with a plastic bag of shit, which he dropped in the trash. A con man, but also a good citizen and conscious of the environment.

Very nice. Time to call it a day, so you roll, stopping at the Arby's down the road for a little repast.

On the way back into the city, Rook thought about how sometimes people were getting it right about life, walking around with those little bags of shit. A metaphor, Sid would call it.

Lucas didn't say anything about Lepke not being in the cemetery when he got back to the garage. Sidney did while they sipped Wild Turkey.

"Hope you didn't waste your time looking for Lepke's grave there," he said. "Lepke is buried in Mount Hebron. Bernard Baruch, the financier, is buried in Flushing. Sometimes I get that switched around since in my head they're kind of interchangeable." He refilled their glasses. "Louis Armstrong is there, too. 'Snakemouth', which was what they called him until some reporter made a mistake which eventually morphed into 'Satchmo', was actually born on August 4, 1901, although Louis always said it was July 4, the year before."

"I appreciate the info," said Rook." I do. 'Lore' you could call it."

"Lore, very good, Lucas boy. Probably from one of the famous research works from the lending library of Sidney Rosen."

"Right, I must have some overdue tomes at my place. I'll check the top of my toilet."

Rook finished his drink and went back to the Saint Claire. First thing he did, was check the messages at his office. Pizzolo calling to see if he had come up with anything. Then Owlsie asking the same, which means Pinto shook his tree, too. Nothing else.

The sofa and the fridge both beckoned. Only a man of sound judgment and courage could handle the challenge. Two pieces of pizza and a cold beverage won out in front of the Yankees, who didn't.

While he brushed his teeth which is very important if you've had a heart trauma, Lucas went over in his head what he had picked up on McGarvey before he drifted off. Whatever crazy shit he dreamt about Etillio whacking his twin brother would be "review of new client information."

Lucas Rook got up at eight and did some cals and shadow boxing. You go for a run now, all the exhaust is going to kill you. Then he went around the corner to start the day's work on the Pinto case over a bagel and coffee. After thinking about the job, there was going to be actually something to do on it. Both were billable. Lucas left a buck tip and went back upstairs.

First thing, was a little homework on shyster, Norman Gibbs, Esquire. Gibbs handled the first work comp case, so maybe an hour's preliminary look at that. Maybe you came up with something you can squeeze the lawyer with if you need him to flush his attorney-client privilege and give up some dirt on

McGarvey. Or if Attorney Gibbs hears that the compo case went to Harvey "My Middle Name is Cash" Weinfeld, maybe he's happy to give you something on the competition.

Then it's taking a look at Weinfeld. Turns out his middle name really is "Cash". Maybe named as a joke by his parents or after that movie, *Cash McCall,* with James Garner and Natalie Wood. Her mysteriously getting dead is the kind of case you should be investigating and not this compo slop.

Weinfeld wasn't stupid, Ryder College and Brooklyn Law School and has his own website to go with his crazy bus advertising. Nothing better than a member of the bar wearing a dealer's eyeshade and handing out money. A list of his big recoveries and a "Ten Commandments for the Injured Worker." Heaven forbid you should also miss out on, "Discounted rates for government employees, former servicemen, members of religious or fraternal organizations and their family members." Of course, Cash hable'd Espanol and had a 24-hour hotline, 800-HAND-JOB or whatever.

Rook called Weinfeld for an appointment.

"My name is Miss Lewis," the voice on the other end said. We look forward to meeting with you." '*We*' probably means an intake person, then maybe a paralegal. A volume practice like that, you're lucky to see an attorney for more than closing the deal.

"I need to see the big guy, today."

"Mr. Weinfeld's in court the entire day."

Sure he is. "Tell Attorney Cash I'm from a union in Newark," Lucas told her. "He sees me today, fine. If not, I'm taking what I got and going up the road."

"Just a minute," Miss Congeniality told him.

A Mr. Menzanotta got on the phone. "I'm the office manager," he said, "Can I help you, Mister…"

You got a male office manager in a law office, you got a defrocked barrister. "Like I told what's her name, I got a bunch of hearing loss cases, plus my own compo, which is my neck and back. You people are interested, we talk, Weinfeld and me. If not, like I said, I'm just going up the road."

"A moment, please, while I check with Mr. Weinfeld's secretary."

"Ninety seconds, Counselor. I feel generous."

Menzanotta got back in forty-five. "Four o'clock today. Mr. Weinfeld is making…"

"Making me spend two hours getting back to Jersey, driving in all the rush hour. Two thirty."

"Two-thirty will be fine. We validate parking. Or we can send our van."

"The van, then. I don't have to put them miles on my Caddy. Cup of coffee and something to read. I'll take the PATH. You can get me at the station."

Rook hung up to show he didn't go for the niceties. Then he got in a little more computer time in, called over to Owlsie to give him an update, and then put on a collar shirt to go with the dago-looking brown leather jacket he got from Muskrat. You're going to meet with a scumbag used to dealing with unions, you got to show him what he wants to see.

The van with the picture of Cash Weinfeld came on time. The coffee was there, but no magazine, which was no biggie because the trip was ten minutes from the PATH. The law office was two storefronts in a strip mall. The receptionist was overweight and wearing lots of that crap jewelry that you see being sold on T.V. The forms for him to sign came from a slimy-looking mope, who cut his nails too short. Rook handed the papers back.

"I told the other guy I wanted to see The Man and he said yes, so I'm out of here," Rook said.

"Albert Menzanotta," said Slimy, offering a handshake that showed his AFL-CIO cufflinks.

He was decked-out like he was taking home some big paper, which means maybe he's partnered-up with Weinfeld or maybe the shop's all his and Cash is just the front.

"Low back and neck, you said. Been to the ER, Mr. Mc Glinchey?"

"I could do that. I'm starting to get pain from this here," said Lucas. "Which is a pain in my ass."

"Radiculopathy. Have you been seen for that?"

"I'm seeing you."

"I mean a medical provider. As our brochure indicates, in New Jersey you have to see a physician approved by your employer's insurance company."

Rook got up. "I want to talk to my lawyer first, before the doctor, which I'm not sure's going to be you people."

"Hold on, Mr. McGlinchey. We're in the service business here. I don't want you dissatisfied."

"I'm talking about more than my comp claim, Alberto. Like I said when I called, I got members who got hearing loss. Which is what I'm either talking to Weinfeld about, who is not here which I am, or I'm taking what I got elsewhere, which looks like I'm going to be doing."

Menzanotta made a call on his cel, and then spoke to his prospective client again, "I reached Mr. Weinfeld. Court adjourned sooner than he expected. He'll be here in twenty minutes. Come into the conference room. Watch ESPN. Have refreshments."

"Dr. Pepper," said Lucas. "If he's on the insurance list."

Forty minutes later, the lawyer showed up. Whoever airbrushed his photo for all those ads was a genius, turning Weinfeld from a typical racetrack degenerate to a man who looked like you could trust him.

"Testimony ran over," he said.

"I'm sure," said Rook.

"How can I be of service?" said Cash Weinfeld.

"Union business in addition to me."

"Unions are at the heart of our great Country, Mr. McGlinchey."

"Right, right. There's a lot of hearing loss claims from the presswork. We're looking for somebody to come out to the hall, do the testing. Handle the claims from soup to nuts. I checked you out. Everybody says you're 'The Man'."

"We have significant expertise in the field," said Weinfeld.

"We'll all make out," said Lucas Rook.

"We do not split fees or anything like that," Menzanotta said.

"Of course, you don't. Maybe you do something for me on my case. Or maybe, I take some photos for you. My local's looking for a home for our people. And there's union elections coming up. You do labor work too, right?"

"We specialize in worker's compensation and personal injury," said Weinfeld.

"Plenty of that. Meanwhile, you hook me up with a doc the insurance is going to pay for, everybody gets well," said Lucas.

"I hope your injuries resolve soon, Mr. McGlinchey," said Weinfeld, and he left the room.

Albert gave Lucas the authorizations and fee agreements to sign and a stack of brochures. Then he wrote a doctor's name and phone number on the back of his card. "You go see Dr. Jackson. He's on their list. Give him my card."

"Will do," said Rook as he scribbled on the forms.

"And then we'll talk about your other needs, Mr. McGlinchey."

"Absolutely."

"I'll have the van take you back," said Menzanotta

"Need an advance. Two, two-fifty," Rook told him.

"We don't do that, Mr. McGlinchey. That's not permitted by our ethics rules here in New Jersey. There is a pair of Net's tickets in your paperwork," he whispered. The shysters were that, but they weren't stupid. Half of their competition paid cash up front in addition to having their sideways deals with the unions, and their runners on the street, which are all crimes. The next time, he'll reel them in, Cash and Company, and put them in Rahway where they belong.

CHAPTER FIVE

Lucas Rook took the van back and then cabbed it over to his office at 166th to check on his mail and messages. The mailman, woman letter carrier, whatever, was finishing Rook's floor when he got off the elevator. She had her hair done and make-up on. Probably playing silver fox to some young puppy that didn't know any better or maybe a long haul trucker whose eyes were failing.

The mail was bullshit, but at least he had a case to run. Lucas hadn't started putting together an initial report yet, but that got moved up a half-day when Pinto called. Ten minutes after, the phone rang again. It was Owls Miksis.

"Pinto Face call you yet today, Rook? The way he was crying to me, if he didn't, he's going to. He's full of it, no doubt about that. But he's a good pay."

"I'm just putting together the first write up. You want it on my paper or yours?"

"Do the report on your letterhead. Send over your billing, which I'll handle. He says when I got something ready, he'll come pick it up."

There was a knock on Rook's door.

"Got to go, Owlsie."

It was the scumbag he met at Judge Schwarzman's office. He had a big legal file under his arm. Lucas opened the door wide and gave Goodwin his badass cop stance.

"Just one moment, please, Mr. Rook, please!"

"That's one too many."

"I'm not a monster. I've got the medical information to prove it from other cases. And I've got plenty of money to pay you."

"The mint doesn't print enough. But I'm doing to do you a favor."

Goodwin started to say something, but the look on Rook's face stopped him.

"The favor I'm going to do because of the Judge, is not throw you out of the window after beating you within an inch of your life for thinking you could just drop your degenerate gambling ass into my place of business, not to mention my apartment building. Nod your head that you understand."

William Goodwin did.

"Now nod your head you understand that I see you again, or hear from you, I don't owe anybody nothing and I'm going to hurt you permanently."

"I understand, Mr. Rook."

"I just heard from you, Billy," Lucas said. "Like I said not to."

Rook feinted with a big right hand. Goodwin flinched, then backed away and left.

Lucas returned to his desk and started Pizzolo's paperwork. No way can you fool a cop who's done a thousand reports himself.

But you don't fancy it up somewhat, he's going to think what you're giving him got bullshit in it anyway.

You write-up what you have, including McGarvey's background, your surveillance and what you've put together with the lawyer and the accident doc. Two hours later, you're done.

Pizzolo's there early, which means he's hoping to find you're not ready or whatever, which would put him one up.

"Your doorman out getting his gold braid cleaned?" said Pizzolo as he sat down. "Give me what you got."

"I got a report, you got an outstanding invoice." Lucas told him.

"No way is the retainer used up. Anyways, that's between me and Miksis."

"What's between you and Owlsie's between you and me," Lucas told him. The he called Owls on the phone and got the okay to hand-over the report.

Pinto Face gave it a quick read. "You're doing your job," he said. "Not that I couldn't have done better."

"You're a regular prince, Pizzolo."

Pinto eyeballed the office. "You didn't have such a fancy address, Fifth Avenue and all, maybe you could have more than this shoebox."

"Love shoeboxes, Phil. So you want to tell me why we are having this face to face?"

"McGarvey. Maybe you take care of that."

Rook gave him a hard look. "My hearing's shot, Phil. Couldn't hear a thing you said."

"You change your mind, you let me know."

"Sure, I won't, Detective Pizzolo."

Pinto stood up. "You do, there's a kicker in it for you."

"Can't hear you, bud," Rook told him. "My ears are way clogged up."

Phil Pizzolo left and Lucas jotted down the time on his billing sheet, and did a bullshit memo at .3. Then he called over to the garage to make another run at McGarvey. You've already been out there once in your Merc, it's either your taking your dead brother's Avanti or Rosen's Jeep or maybe a day rental, if Sid had any.

After rush hour, Rook took a Black Malibu across the 59th Street Bridge for a run out to Queens to give the shitheel another look. Maybe this time you catch him carrying buckets of paint, putting up a ladder, or something else like that, which is going to convince a comp judge he's the scammer he is.

You're at the subject's spot in Flushing. No ladder or paint cans. No dog out on the little balcony. Not much of a balcony either or Freddie McGarvey, unless you're counting the crispy critter being carried out in a body bag.

Lucas flashed ID to the Fire Department's Captain Armella, who was on the scene.

"What we got here, Cap?" Lucas asked.

"Had the space heater too close to the curtains is what it looks like. Dog got toasted too."

"You looking at anything else here?" Lucas asked.

"Not with the budget cuts, I'm not," said Armella.

Rook headed back to Manhattan. Pinto Face Pizzolo just couldn't wait, which explains why he was running his mouth the way he was with what he said. No doubt he already had somebody torch McGarvey, which certainly is one way to close a workers' compensation claim.

Rook dropped the vehicle off at Sid Rosen's.

"You been at a pig roast?" the garage man asked.

"More like a Sam roast. That and my subject, who was named McGarvey. Smells like barbecue, don't it," Rook said.

"That it does, boy. It wasn't so macabre, I'd say it's making me hungry."

Lucas went back to his office and called Owls Miksis, who would price the job right, everything considered. Then he checked around again to follow-up if anybody had come up with work for him. The Esquires, Quinn, Marvin Block, Mel Leibovitz got you zilch. No reason to call Gavilan, who sent you the calendars from Atlanta. He had something, he'd let you know. If Grace Savoy were home when he got back to his place, he'd see if she had any fashion jobs coming up that needed somebody to scare away the pervs.

CHAPTER SIX

Grace was wearing only a pair of green high top sneakers and a cigarette behind her ear when Lucas knocked on her sliding glass door.

"Good morning, neighbor," she said.

"You're sure who this is?" he asked.

She lit up and answered through her exhale of menthol smoke. "You know better," she told him.

"How could I forget, Gracie?" He started and she joined him, "Grace Savoy can hear a pigeon fart a mile away."

The blind supermodel let him in and walked bare-assed into her little kitchen. "Stoli for me. A manly brew for my neighbor man," she said.

"That'll work. You might want to put an apron on or something."

"Actually, Lucas Rook, I was planning to put these cold drinks on my nipples and have them stand up for you."

"I'm sure, Gracie."

She poured herself a double vodka and opened his beer. "It's Iraqi, or something. Made from fermented camel piss, but I get it forever as part of my compensation package."

Lucas took a sip. "Camel piss," he told her.

"Right, "she said as she plopped down on her five thousand dollar couch. A bit of her drink splashed up. "Oh, my heavens, "she said. "I've got Stoli on my perky bosoms. Care for a cocktail?" She took a drag on her cigarette.

"I'm good, Grace."

"You're here for business, not pleasure," she said "Which I understand, even though it was me that saved your life by shooting that black detective with your big and shiny .357 I then threw off the roof. Which then got me charged with manslaughter, which Jake Schwarzman got me out of, which would up with him and me getting each other, if you know what I mean."

Grace Savoy opened her legs. "Hospitable, don't you think?"

"Absolutely. That's just what I would say, Gracie."

"You're not here about my little rabbit, are you neighbor-man?"

"I'm here about anything going on that you need a 'surly', I think you said last time, man to guard your next fashion shoot."

Grace Savoy finished her drink, but held the glass. "I thought perhaps I could use your rock-hard abs as a coaster."

"Not so rock-hard anymore," Lucas said.

"I know a hard man when I feel one," said Grace.

"When it's appropriate," Rook answered. He finished his beer and got up.

"Just a half for me, dear, the Stoli. Help yourself to another can of camel piss if you wish." She took another clutch of menthol and nicotine and stubbed out her smoke. "Yes, yes. Burly and surly. That's you. You sure your lady friend, Catherine, won't mind if we travel together."

"You know Cat's okay that I work for you." He handed her the drink. "I sense a little ball busting here?"

She took a sip and gestured that she wanted another smoke. "On the mantle, dearie," she said. "Of course, I'm busting your shoes a bit, squeezing your shoes, you like to say. How about we talk a little business here? Money, dough, moulah. We all need that, particularly since the world's going to end pretty soon."

"I'm supposed to ask you about that, right Gracie?"

"2012, December 21st is the date it all ends except for me and maybe Jake, if that's the way I want it, Lucas. Maybe you get a pass, too."

"Then I won't have to buy Christmas presents, right?" Lucas said. He handed her a cigarette.

There was a '50's Ronson lighter on the end table and she lit up. "You notice, I did not ask you to do that for me, yes? Part of our complicated dance of interactions."

"I noticed that," said Lucas.

"Three fifty a day and expenses. Save the receipts. They take four weeks to cut the checks. You want me to front it for you, my accountant says I can't, but I will."

"Where we going?"

"No place exotic. Or maybe it is. D.C. They want me in front of that big phallic monument and on Abe Lincoln's lap. White mink and nothing else, of course."

"I can do that," said Lucas.

She smoked her cigarette and finished her drink. "We leave Friday, but you can start the clock earlier if you're available."

"Because why, Grace?"

"Some creepo got on the elevator with me. First he was just there. Then he was talking to me for which I almost tasered him. 'William' he said his name was. Very creepy."

"I don't think he's dangerous, but he is stupid," Rook said. "I'll take care of it, but be careful anyways."

"Okie dokie, Mr. Private Dick. Just keep an eye out. I can't do that you know. He comes around again, fuck him up for me, please. I cannot bear the thought of being assaulted by a creepo."

"You can count on that, Ms. Savoy. Meanwhile, don't worry about that. He's a loser who killed his own kid, so I don't think he'll be bothering you that way."

"We thank you, Lucas. Bunny and I do, that is." She opened her legs again.

Rook ignored it. "You get the particulars, I'm good to go on the D.C. thing."

Lucas Rook went back across the patio to his place. Catherine's train would be coming in an hour. Her conferences always revved her up, the academic politics and whatnot. Last time she was at one, she went on for about a week about Hart Crane and Stephen Crane. No mention of Bob Crane from *Hogan's Heroes*, though, who liked to play kinky and then get beaten to death with his own camera equipment.

Speaking of which, no way young Billy hasn't absolutely earned himself a tune-up. It would have taken maybe five minutes to get Goodwin's particulars from Jake Schwarzman's office, but you're going to beat hell out of the asshole, you don't involve The Swan anyway at all. "Plausible deniability," they call it.

Meanwhile you can get a couple of hours of billables. There's about a hundred hits on Goodwin's situation your surfing the Web turns up, cold medicine, and the like, killing kids. More than a few of the mothers or fathers, no doubt wanted some time without their child so they could hit the casino or bang their boyfriend. Most didn't read the labels.

Rook was at Penn Station early. The train was late. A cup of bad coffee while you watch the bums and the petty thieves and then there's the businessmen looking for VD in the bathroom. Up on the board shows the train from Washington's going to be another forty minutes.

Lucas went over to the MTA Police to see if there was anybody around he knew. The Chinese lady cop asked if she could help him.

"Retired off the job," Lucas told her, which if she was half police, she would have seen a mile away.

"Can I help you?" the Dragon Lady asked with a look that said she had no idea what he just said.

"Looking for an old friend of mine. Must have the wrong tour." And planet maybe.

His cel rang.

"You okay, Cat?"

"We're stuck in a tunnel. It could be hours."

"I'll make some calls," Lucas said. "In the meantime, it's just agro. You're going to be okay. If it was anything more than that, ESU would be there already."

"What does that mean?" she said. Her phone started to beep.

"Save your batteries. I'll be here when you get in," he told her. "You'll be fine."

Lucas called around until somebody gave him that they had sent a repair crew and with luck, it would be another ninety minutes. Then he called Catherine Wren and told her.

"Hour and a half, "he told her. "Maybe sooner. Sweaty's the worst you'll get, Professor."

"I'm glad to hear your voice," Catherine said. "But you really should learn to text."

"Fingers too big for them little keys. I'll be waiting for you."

Rook hung up and took a cab over to his office to bill three hours work in sixty minutes. Then he went back to get the only woman in the world he could imagine himself married to.

CHAPTER SEVEN

Catherine Wren was exhausted after the ordeal on the train and had a Comparative Lit class to teach at Princeton the next morning. More than anything in the world, she wanted a long shower. Then two glasses of white wine out on Rook's patio and sleeping in his arms. That would somehow cancel out his place being a hybrid of a college dorm and a fortress.

In the morning, Lucas rode in the cab with her to Penn Station and then went over to his office at 166 Fifth to check on the mail and to pretend to be working. You've got too much free time, you're sitting in front of the boob tube in your robe. Or you're spending your life in some dive bar, also not good.

The pension check came in the mail, which was good. The knocking on the door from the pain in the ass from the printer's place was not.

"I'm here," Lucas called without getting up.

The pain in the ass came inside. He didn't have the "where's the check look." What he did have, was the "I have done something bad, look."

"Can I speak to you?" he said.

"You're doing that, Lou."

"I mean professionally. You were a New York police detective, weren't you?"

"I was, but you've got to know there's no confidentiality here for what you're saying. That's the law in New York, unless I'm working for a lawyer who's representing you."

"Should I hire one?"

Rook took a bottle of water from the little frig on his right.

"Don't know."

"I, I...."

"Careful, now," Lucas told him. "Remember what I told you."

Louis Skiles sat down and Rook handed him the water. There could be something here if maybe he kidnapped Lindbergh's baby or shot President Kennedy.

"You've been arrested?"

"I might be." He twisted the cap open, but did not take a drink. "For stealing from work."

"Which like I told you, whether you did it, I don't want to know about that."

"We had an audit."

Lucas turned on his clock radio.

"There was money missing," said Skiles. "Almost seven thousand dollars."

Jake Schwarzman would charge that to say hello. Rook opened his drawer and took out his stack of lawyer's cards. He picked-out two who would hire him if they got hired, and wrote the names and phone numbers on the backs of two of his new business cards.

"You go call them, Lou. Now. Tell them I sent you. Pick who you want. You've never been in trouble before this, it'll work out fine. You've been arrested before?"

Skiles shook his head no.

"Okay, then. Call as soon as you leave this room. Just tell them I said you should see them right away. Try and get in today, so your lawyer calls your boss before your boss calls the cops."

"Which lawyer shall I use?"

"They both can handle this. Mike McDermott was with the DA's office. Muldoon was a cop first."

Skiles got up and reached for his wallet.

"We're good here," Lucas told him. "Now remember, the only one you talk to about this is the lawyer. Nobody at work, no friends, like that." Then Rook picked-up the phone to make a pretend call.

The idea of coffee was in his head, and his shoes looked like hell. You can lose out on a client for that. After paying Jimbo Turner a visit, maybe a stop at Muskrat's to complete the trifecta of self-indulgence.

You get a black coffee for yourself and one with milk and two Sweet 'n Low's. Bagel with a schmir and a corn muffin for Jimbo. The shineman was sitting in a chair next to his stand when Lucas came up. He was wearing one of those foot surgery wooden shoes.

"I was just thinking of you, Mr. Rook," said Jimbo Turner. "Thinking you'd come by, with a bag of those fresh Jersey tomatoes."

Rook took out his coffee and bagel and handed Jimbo the bag. "Next best thing, Mr. Turner."

"I guess that be right. A good friend you are to remember a diabetic, old, white shineman." He put the bag down and picked up his brushes. "You carrying around a pound or two of the city dirt and grime. Going to fix these brogans up good." First the brushes, clacking the ends together for the rhythm, clickety clack. Then a coat of the wash which he fanned dry.

Lucas cleared his jacket as two bad guys came across the street.

"Trouble brewing?" Jimbo asked. He reached for the bat that was wedged between his chair and the stand.

"Not for you, my friend," said Rook as the two kept walking.

The shineman went back to work, rubbing in the polish with his fingertips and taking out his rag to start the shine. It snapped like a sail in the wind.

"An artist, Jimbo," said Lucas.

"I appreciate your words," said the shineman as he poured two drops of peppermint oil onto each shoe and then a like amount into his cupped hands. "Keeps the arthritis away," he said as he rubbed them together. He used a piece of nylon stocking to finish the shine.

"See the way your shoes be, you're walking good so you don't need no shoulder to help you down."

"Doing good, my friend," said Lucas.

"Plus, I appreciate you're not talking on this wooden shoe I'm wearing for the trouble from my sugar."

He took the whiskbroom to Rook's jacket and Lucas handed him a fiver and two one's which Jimbo put in his pocket without looking.

"Stay well, Lucas Rook," he said.

"Stay safe, my friend," said Lucas.

"Don't forget them Jersey tomatoes you get a chance," called Jimbo Turner.

Rook walked away and over to Ninth Avenue that used to be a wasteland. Doroshow's knew how to serve a hot roast beef sandwich, dipping the roll in the gravy before serving it up. Some horseradish and a cold tomato and you got it made. He ate, popped a couple of Pepcids, and headed home. Muskrat and his six-dollar shirts were going to have to wait.

Rook let the first two cabs go by, then took the next one back to his place. The front desk called him, "boss" instead of the "sir" that all the others got. Somebody must have let him know about his gold shield and whatnot.

Grace Savoy was waiting for Lucas when the elevator stopped at the top floor.

"You going down?" he asked her.

She did this thing with her hand and her tongue against her cheek that a lady shouldn't.

"Maybe later," Grace said. "I was just coming back from the incinerator chute and could tell the elevator was coming."

"Might not have been somebody as hospitable as me, "Rook said as he started to his apartment.

"And you're not going to invite me in?"

"Give me a couple minutes, Gracie. Radar or whatever, there's no way you're not going to trip over something."

Grace Savoy took a cigarette from the pack in her sock and lit up.

"We wouldn't want that to happen to the most beautiful woman in the world, who is going to employ you on her trip to the Nation's Capitol and also saved your life, now would we?"

"Of course, not," Lucas told her. "But the sooner I get inside, I can make my place something other than a booby-trap."

Grace took a deep drag on her menthol. "Okie doke," she said. "Why don't you stop over to my place and I'll make some martinis and get you to sign the W-9 form and Hold Harmless. Also you can fax over to your liability carrier to add me as an additional insured for the little trip we are going on."

"Anything else?" Lucas asked as he took his key from his door.

She did her obscene imitation of a blowjob again.

CHAPTER EIGHT

Shoko Ashara sat in his maximum-security cell where he had been since his sentence of death by hanging decreed on February 27, 2004. Born poor into a family of floormat makers and afflicted with infantile glaucoma so that he was legally blind, he nevertheless believed himself to be the True Lamb of God.

Ashara had embarked on a career as an acupuncturist after his conviction for practicing pharmacy without a license. He also began his spiritual quest by studying numerous religions and philosophies, including Taoism, Buddhism, Astrology and various forms of Yoga. In 1984, he opened a small studio in his Tokyo apartment.

His organization, Aum Shinrikyo or "The Supreme Truth", began attracting students from local universities and in a period of five years, had expanded so that it received governmental recognition in 1989.

Aum Shinrikyo's growth was as rapid as was Shoko Ashara's embracing of the bizarre. Within a period of three years, he had declared himself, "Christ", and was predicting the coming of Armageddon in which the United States was the Biblical Beast, which would again attack Japan.

Ashara's group continued to grow to a membership of some 10,000 in Japan and almost 50,000 worldwide. When Aum Shinrikyo's attempts at political office failed, it began acquiring military weapons, including a helicopter. It was whispered that they attempted to acquire Russian nuclear bombs through a former KGB agent, Marat Belov.

Aum Shinrikyo then began the manufacture of the nerve agent, sarin, and VX poison gas, as well as acquiring Ebola virus cultures in 1984. This acquisition of chemical and biological weapons was not for posturing or self-defense.

Shoko Ashara directed the use of poison gas on the residents of Japan no less than ten times, beginning on June 27, 1994 when sarin was released in the city of Matsumoto, killing eight and injuring two hundred. With a stockpile of enough of the weapon to kill literally millions of people, Aum Shinrikyou launched a coordinated attack on the Tokyo subway system, resulting in a dozen deaths and an estimated five thousand injuries.

An attempt to kill tens of thousands of others by cyanide gas failed some six weeks later. There also was a massive explosion, which was equivalent to a "major seismic event" on Aum Shinrikyo property that it used as a training site in Australia.

A decade passed before Japanese authorities dismantled the doomsday cult and its godhead was arrested. Shoko Ashara was found guilty of thirteen of seventeen charges and was sentenced to the gallows. Three appeals of the death sentence were denied and an attempt by Marat Belov to free Ashara failed.

Aum Shinrikyo was brought to its knees with numerous other arrests and convictions and the loss of the organization's protected status. Eventually bankrupt, it was succeeded by a new group, which declared its name to be *Aleph,* the first letter of the Hebrew language, standing for the concept of "Beginning".

Aleph apologized for the activities of its predecessor and promoted itself as a purely religious and educational organization. Its website announced, "Liberation of Soul, The Age of Benevolence." Then came the creation of the Tau.

Taking its name from the last letter of the Hebrew alphabet, "The Last shall be the First," each member wore the cross-like symbol of the letter. Other than Marat Belov and Oleg Kutzenov, known as "Edmund Brodeur," none of the Tau knew that they were little more than a tool for the Russian front organization, The Foundation.

The Russian hatred of the Japanese was more than a century old and the desire to avenge their loss of the 1904-05 war was still present. Added to this, was the long running disputes over the Kurul Islands, which affected tens of thousands of square miles of economically significant ocean. President Medvedev had ordered significant reinforcement of the Russian defenses on the islands, consistent with the fact that the two nations were still legally "under a state of war."

More importantly, there was Russia's need to respond to Japan's growing imperialism, which was manifesting itself in an ever-increasingly advanced air force and navy. The even more threatening Asiatic enemy, China, also needed to be shown that Mother Russia deserved respect.

For these reasons, The Foundation was created to deal with "The Problem". This clandestine operation posing as a think-tank for economic cooperation directed the actions of Marat Belov, and Oleg Kutzenov-Edmund Brodeur. It also employed Dr. Teriyuki Mauritani.

There had been over thirty million people in range of the Fukashima Nuclear Reactor and the Tokyo Electric Power Company was ill prepared to deal with what awaited it. This was despite the fact that it had a history of serious nuclear accidents going back more than three decades. As a result, Dr. Mauritani's attack of March 11, 2011 killed thousands. Millions were displaced and exposed to radiation.

It began with the 9.0 earthquake he created. As the earth trembled and cracked, Mauritani's tsunami was born. Thousands of bodies washed up on the Miyagi shores. The crematoria were overloaded. And then the Fukashima Reactor exploded.

On March 11, Japanese Prime Minister Kan declared a nuclear emergency because of the damage to the nuclear plant, and the following day, he inspected it himself. Despite the venting of radioactive steam from No. 1 reactor, a hydrogen explosion rocked the building, causing the evacuation zone to be expanded to a twenty-kilometer radius.

Two days later, another explosion occurred, this time in No. 3 reactor's building. Then the fuel rods in reactor No. 2 were exposed. The following day, there was another explosion at reactor No. 2 and one at No. 4.

Repair workers were forced to flee for fear that there was such damage that a Chernobyl event was possible. Japanese Self-Defense Forces began using helicopters to douse the facility, as the effort of fleets of fire trucks and the injection of seventy tons of water was insufficient to prevent the temperature in the reactor facility from rising. Thousands of fuel rods were exposed and began melting. There were more than one hundred aftershocks.

The poisonous spread of radioactivity continued so that eight days after the attack, there were significant levels found in milk and spinach as far away as Ibaraki.

There were such high levels of radioactive iodine in Tokyo's water supply, that the government urged that tap water not be given to infants. The levels in the water near the reactor were almost 2,000 times the allowable level. Sea life began to exhibit radioactivity.

The power plant was far from secured even when it was announced as such. And there still remained the long-term damage to the country's economy and the risk of thyroid and bone cancers and leukemia. The horror that also poisoned the minds of the Japanese was like that from the American atomic bombs so many years ago.

After months of internal evaluation Russia's GRU, the Main Intelligence Directorate, met with the SVR, the Russian Foreign Intelligence Service. Together they agreed upon once again implementing the genius of Dr. Mauritani. The Foundation was appropriately directed and accordingly, sent Marat Belov to begin negotiations, or if necessary, to terminate the esteemed scientist.

As he was directed, Belov went to the modest home of Dr. Teriyuki Mauritani.

"May I help you?" asked the man at the door in his housecoat and slippers.

"You should have been expecting me," said the Russian.

"There must be some mistake, sir. I am retired."

"As you say, Doctor. Perhaps you will remember me when I come back another day."

"No need for you to return to my quaint house on this turning street. I do seem to remember your face. A student of mine at the University, I think. Do come in."

Mauritani stood aside so that his guest might enter and led him to the small sitting room on the left. "No need to bring a weapon when you call upon your old professor," he said.

Belov let the comment pass. It had been many years since he went on such a visit unarmed and he wore his SIG Sauer in the pancake holster at the small of his back with the ease of an accountant wearing a tie.

Mauritani gestured for his guest to sit and took the soft chair for himself.

"Are you available?" asked the visitor.

"I am retired, sir, as I told you. I need to rest and enjoy the comforts of these United States."

"You will not have to travel, and I will supply such assistance as you may require, Dr. Mauritani. The entire World will remember your work. Even more than Tokyo."

The professor waited.

"Five million dollars," said Marat Belov.

"Where?" asked Mauritani.

"Washington, D.C. This nation's capital. First yours, now theirs."

The professor closed his eyes. "Ten," he said.

"Six".

"Eight million. I'm tired after my last work," said Mauritani.

"7.5, subject to the approval of my superiors. In three equal payments. The third upon completion."

"Like a house painter or carpenter. How quaint. You may let yourself out. I will be moving soon. You will have to find me. Or your 'superiors' whoever they may be."

The Tau had taken-over the former residence of a Hare Krishna group in the Mt. Airy section of the city. Lots of vegetarians, yoga studios, coffee shops and a food co-op. "Hide in plain sight." had always been a serviceable approach.

The three-story building on Wayne Avenue contained six bedrooms, a large kitchen, two small offices, a communal dining room and on the third floor, a prayer room. There was a large yard in the rear for their compost heap and garden.

Anna Lamb met Edmund Brodeur at the door as he returned from his meeting at the Foundation where he was Oleg Kutzenov. She had come to The Tau from California, where her name was Barbara Horowitz. Anna touched the symbol of the Tau she wore around her neck on a leather cord. Then she did the same for the infant she carried in the sling close to her breast.

"We are blessed to have you here," she said.

Brodeur touched the larger wooden symbol he wore. "There is only one true Savior, and he is The True Lamb of God, who was sent to us to cleanse our sins."

She pulled the bell rope that hung to her right and Scott Lamb came down the stairs. He was as blonde as she was dark.

"You must be tired from your trip, Brother Brodeur," he said. "May I offer you some refreshment?"

"A glass of spring water would be nice. I shall be in my office," Brodeur answered. "I will lead the evening prayer."

"A great blessing," said Anna

Oleg Kutzenov started up the wide wooden steps, and then turned around. "The alarm was not on when I arrived. The Tau welcomes all who come in peace, but one should be neither so prideful nor lazy as not to protect the flock."

He went into his office and locked the door. The business records of the group were there, contributions, income and expenses. He perused them before arranging the pillows so that he might lie down. After his rest, Brodeur met with Scott Lamb to discuss the day-to-day activities.

"The record shop is doing well, Brother," Scott said.

"Not well enough to support the house and the outreach we discussed. Prayer services and charitable work are very important," Brodeur told him, touching his amulet. "However, we do need revenue to sustain ourselves."

"The new member of our flock, John, gave a gift of five thousand dollars."

"Most generous of him. And a blessing to his own heart," said Brodeur.

Scott Lamb touched the holy place between his eyes and the wooden amulet.

"How is he?" asked Brodeur.

"Eager to work and to please, although he is quite concerned about the impending doom that the unsanctified are saying is coming."

"I shall counsel him to accept the comfort of our Blind Messiah," said Brodeur.

Scott Lamb touched the symbol of the Tau again "*Ba-Abba*," he said.

"Our Father is coming," answered Edmund Brodeur.

A bell rang downstairs, which meant it was time for the meal. The food was plain, but good. Squash soup, seitan and vegetables, rhubarb pie. They ate slowly and in silence.

Brodeur spoke when they were done. "Your meal was nourishing, as our work should be. And both bring sustenance to our Family, blessed by Our One True Savior."

Then Kutzenov led the evening devotionals, addressing their newest member's concern with the predicted apocalypse of 2012, and reminding his members of The Tau that their Blind Messiah would protect them.

"*Ba-Abba*," they said in unison, touching the cross-like letter Tau they each wore.

After prayers, Brother Brodeur met privately with John Lamb, who told him that his wife and young son had died and he was so thankful for his new family. His new spiritual leader offered comfort and blessings. William Goodwin wept and went to the prayer room as he was directed.

Three days later, Oleg Kutzenov met in Boston, with his contact from The Foundation. "I did not know that you appreciated ice hockey," he said to Reba Nemerov.

"My brother played at home," she answered. "Even so, I have never been to the Boston Garden before." She unbuttoned her coat. "Would you buy me a beer, please? 'To strengthen and spread democracy and economic liberalization'," she said, quoting The Foundation's credo. "Or then again, sometimes, one is just thirsty."

They stayed through the first two periods of the Bruins game and then left with the home team comfortably ahead by two goals. Brodeur walked Reba Nemerov to her car, where she allowed a kiss on the cheek for appearance sake. In their brief embrace she passed him a disk the size of a nickel on which were encrypted The Foundation's directions.

CHAPTER NINE

Grace Savoy had negotiated a stretch limo and driver as part of the package for her D.C. fashion shoot and passed it on to Lucas Rook. "You don't even have to wear one of those fancy chauffeur's hats, dear," she said, "And I do need a real limousine, and not one of those claustrophobic Lincolns or Cadillacs or whatever they are."

"Whatever you want, Gracie, although those Towne Cars got plenty of room."

"I have what I want, dear." She lit a cigarette. "If Lawrence acts so bitchy as only he can, director or not, you slap him for me."

"Absolutely."

"I love it," she said as she took another hit on her Kool, and said "goodbye" or something in a foreign language.

Lucas called over to Owls Miksis to see how Pinto was doing in paying his bill, which if he doesn't pay Owlsie, you don't get paid.

"He's up to date, Rook. I can wait and pay you all at once or on what I got now."

Lucas hung his shirt over the chair so he would get another wear out of it. "I could use the cash while I'm finishing things up."

"Done," said Owls. "I could mail it or you could ride out here."

"Mail's okay," said Rook. "Appreciate it."

So now that you got that it's way more likely than not that Phil Pizzolo had the scummer, McGarvey burnt up, you're going to bang him on your billing, which he's going to pay because he knows what you're thinking. Also, you're going to write your report like it could be a roadmap for testimony later. You didn't see anything, hear anything like those three monkeys. Pizzolo will be happy to pay for that extra touch.

The phone rang. It was Sid Rosen. "You do me a favor, Lucas boy?"

"What you got, Sidney?"

"Going out to see the old lady this weekend. The grandson's going to be there. He doesn't like dogs. His mother, my wife's kid, don't neither. You look after Bear for me? He doesn't do well in those kennels."

"Going on a job, Sid, for which my client got herself that stretch limo."

"That's show biz, kid," said Rosen.

"You alright?" Lucas asked.

"Bear, he'll like the ride out to Long Island anyway. I should bring the old lady a pie or something. You going out, grab me a lemon meringue. Then maybe we'll share a libation."

Sid was in his early seventies. He could still diagnose car trouble like he was psychic and did all his own mechanical work. Plus, he was smart enough to see his wife on weekends and then, not every one. He never asked you for much, so you add pie to your list of to-do's.

"I got some paperwork to bang out," Lucas said. "Then I'll be by."

Rook put his shirt back on and went up to the office to finish his report and bill. The 3 x 5 cards were gone since he found out about the barbeque where McGarvey was the main course. There was nothing in the computer to worry about.

Maybe five minutes after Lucas was at his desk, the printing thief knocks on the door. Unless he's going by some time-warp calendar, he's still not getting his check for the printing job.

"I just wanted to say thank you, Mr. Rook, for recommending the attorney, Mr. McDermott, I really couldn't afford Mr. Muldoon. He said everything would work out. I feel confident with him."

"You do what he tells you," Lucas told him.

Louis said, 'Thank you' and nothing about his bill and kept nodding his head until he left the one room office, which allowed Lucas Rook to get back to work.

In McGarvey's final report, you got the claims history surveillance, what medical there is and the investigator's observations. Also, photos and Hobe's report, which you redact the shit out of, so no way it traces back on him, and some legal mumbo jumbo right out of the Internet. The shyster comp lawyer gets included, but not so you're giving him any ammo to sue you. Your conclusion doesn't mention about how McGarvey got dead.

Rook did the bill twice to get whatever he could from Pinto Face's bankroll. Pizzolo's half a con man himself, but he's no pussy by any means. So despite what he thinks you think about the fire, he's going to try and get you to cut the bill, which is why you got some bullshit in there for him to take out.

Bottom line is you want to walk away with $2,000 net plus your expenses, and Owlsie's got to be paid. Also you want Pinto Face to know not to fuck with you, so the figure you come up with is $6,750, which is telling him five grand, is as low as you'll go.

You're done, you go down the hall for some deep concentration on the porcelain throne. When you're back, your answering machine is blinking. It's your crazy blind neighbor, Grace Savoy talking like that fat black woman on *The Wire,* who says her gangster-wannabe son "be acting a bitch," except she's talking about Lawrence. The producer, director, whatever, was busting her balls again, probably because he wished he didn't have any. Gracie says the shoot is off. Fifteen minutes later the phone rings again. "Everything's fine," she said. "Just fine."

"You sure?" he answered.

"Artistic differences. We're resolved them."

"Good."

"I informed him that you would fuck his shit-up. So thank you, Lucas Rook. Private detectively speaking, you be the bomb in PP, which means 'personal protection', which Jake is gracious enough for him to use that in our little get-togethers."

"Way too much info there, Gracie," Lucas said. "Now, I got to get back to what I'm doing here."

"Fucking somebody up?"

"Kind of," Rook told her.

It took another hour and a half to get things right. When the bill was done, Lucas called Owls, who was taking a siesta. Not a bad idea, but there's places to go, people to see. Which means the pie and Muskrat because you're going to be working with a high-fashion model, you can't look like a schleper, even if she's blind as a bat.

You cab over to his place that is still in the Fashion District, although there's not much of that left. He's got prices that make discount look like Barney's. There's a new Puerto Rican running the freight elevator up, except he's Mexican. With Muskrat, this means he's probably getting him for four bucks an hour instead of five.

Muskrat was covered with hair everywhere, which is how he got his name. This time, he was looking all puffy. "Detective, detective," Muskrat said, but not getting up from his chair. "You needing some more of those tropicals you got last time?"

Lucas walked over. The closer he got, the worse Muskrat looked.

"What can I do for you, detective?"

"Going to be around a lot of fashion types."

"Sunny climes?"

"D.C."

"Roberto, see what we got in suits. Gray, I'm thinking. If not, black, 48's and 50."

Lucas leaned against the desk. "Got my funeral suit," he said. "I'm thinking a raincoat, you know, 'trench coat' we used to call them."

"And bedroom slippers, you need those. And maybe five or six dress shirts. Half with French cuffs. And silk ties, six of them, Roberto. *Comprende?"*

The Mexican brought over what was called out to him and a bathrobe. Rook got the raincoat, two shirts and a necktie, which was about as likely to be silk as it was ever to be worn at all.

"Going to be having a big sale," Muskrat called as Lucas got on the freight elevator. "Biggest one you ever saw."

So another one's got the Big C. Muskrat, he'll probably pick a cardboard coffin. Have his own funeral for fifty bucks.

The German accent on the other end of the phone at midnight meant either that the Nazi's had landed again, Rosen had told him that a U-boat did that in June of 1942 in East Hampton, or it was crazy Grace from across the way.

"Did I wake you, neighbor?" she asked.

"It's fine, Gracie. Nothing better than Hitler in the middle of the night."

"Wouldn't you like to take me to breakfast before we leave?"

Lucas turned on the lamp on his night table.

"I'm supposed to say, 'where', right, Gracie? Like knock-knock. I'm going to take a leak, after which, call me if it's not a joke, which I'm hoping it is. Otherwise, I'm going back to sleep."

"Okie, dokie," she said. "Drain that vein, water your dragon, and shake the snake. You having prostate problems waking you up, I can help you with that."

The phone rang again while he was still in the bathroom. Rook picked it up on the sixth ring.

"That was quick," he said.

"I thought you might have a phone in your *loo*. Jake has one."

"That's nice, Grace. Elegant or something."

"He has three in his limousine," Gracie said. "Also, they're moving up the shoot. Something about not having to pay overnight rate for the union. Today's the first one. We can go grab something scrumptious or I can make you waffles."

"I'll pass on the breakfast."

"And then I can read them to you. The waffles, I mean."

"If you're serious, I'm still going back to sleep, Ms. Savoy."

"I am. I mean I was. It was off. Now it isn't, so we're to leave at five thirty AM. Jake is sending his limousine and his driver."

Lucas set his alarm for five so he could catch a couple of hours. Then he had a cup of black coffee, dressed for the job and went downstairs. The limo was there and the doorman and the driver were catching a smoke.

"Mr. Rook, I'm Ms. Savoy's driver."

"You got ID?" Rook asked him.

"Duane Carrington." He took out his wallet and showed his license. "The Judge said you'd want to see this."

"You been with him long?"

"When he calls, I'm there. I was a teamster in Newark and worked security." He finished his smoke. "Played a little football before that."

Lucas walked around the car and looked under it.

"You want me to pop the trunk?" asked the driver.

"And the hood, too."

Carrington took another deep draw on his Marlboro. "Serious, aren't you?"

"As a heart attack, my friend," Rook told him.

"I've driven the Judge a couple of years," said Carrington. "No problems."

"You do what I ask you, we'll do just fine." Lucas said and went back upstairs.

Grace Savoy was waiting at her door when he got off the elevator.

"I'm ready to roll," she called.

"Three minutes," he told her, "And you should be in your apartment."

"I've got to pee, too, Mr. Lucas Rook. And don't forget to wear clean undies just in case we have a car wreck and everybody's killed."

Rook went inside and checked the traffic on his computer. Then he checked his weapons that he could carry thanks to President Bush signing The Law Enforcement Safety Act. Before that, D.C. was impossible. You're carrying illegal could cost you ten grand. Still, you had to be careful being around the museums and the like, whether you got your 218 permit or not.

Lucas opened his door to get Grace Savoy and she's standing there.

"Quiet as an Indian, huh?" she said.

"Right, Gracie. You're waiting like I told you not to. Where are your bags?"

"Duane came up and got them."

Lucas shook his head.

"Wait in here, Grace, my place."

She leaned against the doorframe and reached for a cigarette from the pack she kept in her sock. "You mind?" she asked.

"Going to check the vehicle again," he told her. "Do like I said."

"I mean, if I smoke in your place."

"Knock yourself out," he said. "Just don't burn holes in my sofa. And do not unlock the door."

Rook went back down the elevator and over to the limo.

"You think I checked-out your vehicle for the fun of it?" he asked Carrington.

"She has lots of bags," said the driver. "The doorman...."

"Right. Don't even say anything about the doorman. You left the vehicle unattended."

Lucas was checking the limousine again when his cel rang.

"I'm still ready," she said a second time.

"Two more minutes. Do not move. I'm coming up to my apartment to get you."

"How perfectly professional, Lucas Rook," she said.

"Absolutely."

"*Auf Wiedersehen*," said Grace Savoy.

"*Gesundheit*," he told her and hung up.

She called back. "It means, 'seeing you again'. It was important for me to say that. I am blind, you know."

"Foreign languages aren't my strong suit, Grace."

"Seeing you again," she said and she hung up.

Rook finished what he had to do and went to get his client. When they got to the curb, Grace Savoy walked over and waited for someone to open the door for her. Carrington made a big show of his going to help her. Lucas went and stood in front of them.

"Okay, folks. I'm going to say this once and just once. This may not be a big deal for you, and maybe it isn't at all, except for me, but from this moment on until we're down to D.C. and back, the two of you do exactly what I tell you. You don't agree to that, Duane over here can do the driving and my job. Tell me right now."

"Right now," said Grace. "Yes, sir. For both of us."

"Let me hear it, Carrington," said Lucas.

"What she said. Absolutely."

"Okay, people," said Grace Savoy. "Now let's get the party started."

They went through the Holland Tunnel onto the New Jersey Turnpike. Carrington did a good job driving.

"Would you like to stop, Ms. Savoy? There's a Roy Rogers in the rest stop up ahead," he asked.

"Fried chicken and biscuits, my favorite breakfast, Kenny. And you know how much I love that cardboard holster and the French fries. But I think I'll wait. Meanwhile, I'm going to get a little beauty sleep, which for me is hardly necessary."

"Okay, then," said the driver.

"I don't have to close my eyes to sleep, you know, fellows. But I will, so it's not too creepy."

CHAPTER TEN

After the Foundation's woman left, Oleg Kutzenov did not go back into the Arena to watch the Bruins finish off the Flyers, who were trying out another new goalie. A couple leaving early when the home team was ahead certainly would draw less attention than his coming and going, then coming back again. Even with the use of increasingly more sophisticated technical advances, it was his unwavering commitment to his craft that allowed Kutzenov to successfully work with the Russians, The Tau, and the Blind Messiah.

After, Edmund Brodeur rode the MBTA to Logan Airport where he boarded the plane as Bernard Marcu. The disk given to him had his new instructions, which included that his next meeting would take place three thousand miles away.

His airfare to San Francisco was expensive as he was booking only the day before and because the route there necessarily was circuitous and with multiple plane changes. Fortunately, Kutzenov was used to resting in taxis, airplanes and airports, so that when he arrived at the Holiday Inn on Columbus Avenue via the BART rail line from SFO, he merely showered and changed his clothes to meet Teriyuki Mauritani outside the Yang Sing restaurant in San Francisco.

They walked through Chinatown, in and out of several shops, exchanging questions and answers in French, Mandarin and German and parted company without a goodbye. Brodeur took his flight back to the East Coast via Houston and Chicago.

Dr. Mauritani stayed another day enjoying the sights, particularly, Alcatraz as the fog separated. Then he went back to complete his calculations, which would take all his knowledge and skill in physics, geology, and his special understanding of earthquakes.

Upon his arrival home, he learned that the first installment of his payment had been deposited in his numbered account in Switzerland. Mauritani boiled some water for a cup of bancha tea. What a strange place Washington D.C. was. All of the governmental and political power doing evil. The lobbyists, the corrupt businessmen, the bankers, the spies, the military, the pompous Negro president who was so immature and self-absorbed. It all would be washed away.

Dr. Mauritani boarded the twenty-dollar New York to Washington, Chinatown bus on Allen Street. No longer was he the renowned physicist who had brought Japan to its knees, but another old Asian man taking cheap transportation.

He got off at the stop on H Street, walked in and out of some shops, and then changed taxis before a trip by metroliner to the National Airport, now named after the cowboy actor and president, Ronald Reagan. A rental car was waiting for him under another the Korean name, Peter Cho, and he made the thirty-five mile trip to the Chesapeake quite easily, contrary to the racist observation that Asian drivers were all dangerous incompetents.

Dr. Mauritani chose a Holiday Inn a little more than eight miles from his destination, although he certainly could have afforded the Wellington or the Chesapeake Beach Hotel. He awoke at 5 AM and made the quick ride to the Ronald B. Greene Marina, where he became but one of the hopeful fishermen aboard the forty-two foot party boat, Aunt Isabel. A Washington Redskins cap and sunglasses to block the glare off of the water were his only camouflage, sufficient because it shielded his face and simultaneously announced he was "a real American."

Chesapeake Bay is the largest estuary in the United States, surrounded by Virginia and Maryland, and once was a fisherman's haven. But an overgrowth of algae caused by farming and industrial waste had resulted in hypoxia, a lethally reduced amount of oxygen in the water, which destroyed the shellfish population. Additionally, years of unchecked pollution had made the Chesapeake's prized striped bass inedible. The stripers, however, were making a comeback lately and there were enough bluefish, drums and Cobias to interest the twenty-five other fishermen. Mauritani, however, was much more interested in topography than the fish.

Teriyuki Mauritani began his education at Nihon University, the largest university in Japan. He was an undistinguished student in the College of Science and Technology, while Dr. Kiyoo Mogi was already a world-renowned expert on volcanoes and earthquakes, particularly as to what was called, "The Pacific Ring of Fire" because of the more than four hundred and fifty volcanoes contained there.

Mauritani followed Mogi to the University of Tokyo, previously The Imperial University, where the revered expert continued to receive acclaim and adulation for his Mogi Doughnut Hypothesis and his various other postulates on earthquakes, plate tectonics, and volcanoes. So great was his expertise and fame, that Dr. Mogi became known as the World's foremost predictor of earthquakes, and was named Director of the Earthquake Research Institute.

Teriyuki Mauritani eventually became assistant professor in the University's Graduate School of Science, having received his PhD in superconductivity. What brought him to the study of earthquakes, however, was not academics or science, but baseball. Both Mauritani and Mogi were avid fans of the game and particularly of Aka-Oni, the "Red Devil".

Aka-Oni was born, Charlie Manuel, in the back of an automobile in Virginia. His father, a Pentecostal preacher who lived out of a suitcase, became so despondent at his inability to provide for his family, that he committed suicide. Charlie had to turn down a basketball scholarship to The University of Pennsylvania in order to support his mother. When their situation improved a bit, he was able to leave his hometown to play baseball, which also generated some income.

After a stint in the minor leagues where he demonstrated a prowess for hitting a baseball great distances, Charlie pursued a successful career in Japan, hitting .316 with forty-two home runs for the Yokut Swallows in 1977. In 1979, Aka-Oni was hit in the face by a pitched ball, some say to prevent him from breaking a long-standing homerun streak. The pitch thrown by Soroku Yagisawa, broke Manuel's jaw in six places.

After numerous complex surgeries, the big American still managed to return that season, and lead his team to their first pennant, much to the pleasure of his fans, Drs. Teriyuki Mauritani and Kiyoo Mogi, who followed his career in the US where he won many games and a World Series as manager of the Philadelphia Phillies.

Despite the difference of almost a dozen years in their ages, the two had become close friends, spending evenings drinking cold bottles of Kirin beer in front of the televised baseball game or debating whether or not Eiji Sawamura did strike out Charlie Gehringer, Babe Ruth, Lou Gherig and Jimmie Foxx in succession. The friendship between Mogi and Mauritani eventually resulted in Mauritani being brought into the Earthquake Research Institute, where the pay was better and the science greatly appreciated.

While Teriyuki's training did not allow him the spotlight that his mentor enjoyed, it did educate him in the science and protocol of earthquake experiments, including those that were conducted as far back as 1893, which was a controlled attempt to create a tidal wave in an indoor pool. Project Seal was much more than that.

On December 18, 1950, The Department of Scientific and Industrial Research of Wellington, New Zealand issued the top-secret report, "Project Seal". The report was authored by Professor T.D.J. Leech of the School of Engineering of Auckland University in Ardmore, New Zealand and chronicled the joint efforts of the New Zealand Armed Forces and the United States Navy from 1944 to 1946. The purpose of those efforts was to investigate and develop the creation of tidal waves as an offensive weapon of war.

Project Seal originated from the experience of Wing Commander EA Gibson of the New Zealand Air Force while he was engaged in blasting operations as part of surveys in the Pacific from 1936 to 1947. Commander

Gibson noted that when explosive charges were used on coral formations as part of that survey, larger than expected waves were produced. He thereupon reported his findings to General Edward Patties, Chief of the New Zealand General Staff, who brought them to Admiral Bill Halsey, U.S. Commander of the South Pacific. Admiral Halsey requested that the joint U.S.-New Zealand project be undertaken, beginning in April of 1944.

The fortress at Whangaparao Peninsula in the Hauraki Gulf in New Zealand was chosen to house the experiment because of its favorable location, not only from a security standpoint, but also because of its proximity to Auckland and appropriate bodies of water, both internal pools and the open ocean.

Dr. Leech then undertook the experiments despite the fact that his consultations with English and American scientists had yielded mixed responses. More than thirty-five hundred such experiments were held between June 6, 1944 and January 8, 1945. The explosives utilized ranged from .06 lb to 600 lbs in weight and though largely utilizing TNT, also included E nitro-starch and gelignite. Wave lengths, hydraulics, energy output, amplitude and dispersion were measured.

Unfortunately, pre-conceived pessimism by certain scientists, internal and external politics, and changes in military priorities resulted in delay and interference with the project. This was despite the conclusion of Professor Leech, later approved by Admiral Halsey, that the creation of tidal waves as an offensive weapon "has definite and far reaching possibilities."

It took more than six years for the report to be completed. By then, World War II had long been over and the Project was reduced to academia, even when the report was declassified on October 21, 1971.

Dr. Teriyuki Mauritani however, had combined those findings with his own expertise and the teachings of his mentor to produce viable plans for his attack on Tokyo and now on, Washington D.C. Both were presented to the Foundation for its approval.

The Foundation also considered, but rejected Marat Belov's recommendation for action. An appropriate detonation in the chosen volcano would cause a half million tons of rock to fall and release an explosion of trapped superheated seawater. This would result in a mega-tsunami with enough power to reach the East Coast of the United States.

However, as Dr. Mauritani's critique of Belov's proposal indicated, there was also the possibility of failure caused by a potential landslide into the sea and the gradual release of pressure by the very porous lava and the open basaltic layers. The Foundation much preferred Mauritani's approach, because of its simplicity and the history of tidal waves near the Atlantic Coast. An induced undersea landslide there would cause unstable sections of the continental shelf to collapse into the trenches of the deep ocean. This would result in a deadly wall of water that would impact Washington, D.C. in only a few hours.

Tidal waves had been present on the East Coast going back to "The Great Swell in the Delaware" in 1849, the tidal wave of January 9, 1926 in Maine, and one in Atlantic City in 1981. Most recently, there were tremors in Virginia and an earthquake struck Gaithersburg, Maryland in July 2010. The Chesapeake was the perfect place to launch a Tsunami Bomb. It would be the responsibility of the Foundation to see that the HMX explosives he had selected were untraceable and stored upon the fishing boat, both relatively simple tasks.

Despite the fact that his mind was on explosions and tidal waves, Mauritani managed to win the pool for "first catch" on the Aunt Isabel, when the sea-robin caught by the dentist next to him was disqualified as a trash fish and therefore not eligible. The largest fish prize went to a big bald man named, Ed Chrissie, who had a little brown and white dog with him, that sat motionless at his feet, except for the roll of the boat on the green waves.

CHAPTER ELEVEN

Brodeur's flight from Boston to Philadelphia was easy, but the transportation to the Tau's home in the Northwest part of the city required two trains, the second old and odiferous. However, as always, he was treated with reverence when he arrived at the three-story structure. He unpacked his bag and reviewed the mail that included the criminal records check that he ordered on William Goodwin, as was his practice with any new member.

The report was a bad one. Involuntary manslaughter of his own child. The Foundation would either instruct him to banish John Lamb or perhaps allow his use as a scapegoat in the upcoming action.

After dinner, there was the regular business meeting before the evening prayers. Brother Brodeur suggested that they engage in a social activity that would not only strengthen their bond, but also provide healthful recreation. He suggested a group outing bus ride, during which they could sing and play word games, and then communing with nature and generating some income with a half-day fishing trip.

The idea was accepted with only some concerns from Scott Lamb, who did not want to subject their infant to the germs of strangers. Kutzenov-Brodeur kept an eye on William Goodwin, who as usual, seemed shy, but willing to participate and follow directions. The rest of the group seemed happy and eager for their little adventure.

The following day, Edmund Brodeur visited the record store they operated on Emlen Avenue. There was a public school in walking distance and there had been two incidents recently from unruly students. One was merely mischief, but the other involved shoplifting. Left unchecked, this would no doubt lead to more. An alarm system had been rejected by the group and likely, the Fourteenth Police District wouldn't have time for this type of crime.

He spent two hours in the store with John Lamb. The only visitor was a short black man from the neighborhood, who looked at some Otis Redding albums and left.

Scott Lamb led the evening prayers for the Tau. There were sufficient pamphlets from which to draw his brief sermon. He chose one of the homilies about education, being careful in his preparation to include the two other standards on which their organization was founded, "Sustenance" and "Scientific Spirituality."

Then the Tau adjourned for their brief business meeting. It was announced that the Mt. Airy Food Co-op had agreed to purchase their squash after completing an investigation of the growing process. This had first appeared problematic because of inorganic run off from their neighbors' yards.

The news drew applause and Anna Lamb even held up her baby, Ariel, who flailed her arms and legs for the brief time she was not comforted by her mother.

The last of the "new business" was the fishing trip they would be taking. It had been a very long time since all of them had left the house together and there were questions about the expense. But Franklin Lamb presented the information given to him from Brodeur, including that the bus ride had been donated and that with the box lunches they would bring, the cost would be negligible, being only the charge for their seats on the fishing boat. And further, if they had any luck at all, they could actually make money. The striped bass would be fresh caught, which the Co-op had also agreed to buy.

After the evening's group activities were completed, Scott, Anna, and Ariel went for a walk in the early evening air, down Wayne Avenue and onto the Lincoln Drive.

"I didn't want to say anything in the house," said Anna. "But Ariel is due for her booster shot the day before the trip and it may make her feverish."

"Or more," said Scott Lamb. "Where do you think all this autism comes from? I thought we had spoken about this."

"We have. I do respect your concerns for our child. However, I also do not wish her to get pertussis. Whooping cough can kill Ariel. There could be nothing worse."

He took a deep breath and slowly exhaled. Then another.

"Okay," he said. "I am concerned, but I shall pray our Lamb of God will protect her."

When they got to the corner of Johnson Street, they turned around.

"I'm sorry I got upset," said Scott. "We could have gone to Kathie's School and taken Ariel on the swings."

Anna put her hand on his arm. "Next time," she said. "Besides, our little angel is asleep."

William Goodwin went to Scott Lamb when he returned from his family walk. "If you wish, I could go to the drugstore and get Dramamine. I have learned all about the benefits of over the counter drugs."

Scott Lamb took his hands and pressed on a spot three inches above each wrist. "This will do," he said. "And I will bring ginger root. As Shoko Ashara, our one true Father has said, 'Nature is the provider and the cure.'"

"I will remember that," said Goodwin. "But what of the Apocalypse that is coming on December 21st, the geomagnetic reversal, the polar shift…"

"The Spirit of Love that comes from our Blind Messiah has saved you, John Lamb. And he will protect us all. "*Ba-Abba,* Father is coming."

There were morning prayers at sunrise, inviting their True Father to send his love. Then each member of the Tau had their work to do before breakfast, then the communal meal of brown rice and raisins, and home-baked bread with soy butter. The house smelled sweet from the baking.

William Goodwin walked to their record store. It was between an Indian take-out restaurant and the office for the Philadelphia Folk Society. There used to be a fancy antique dealer on the corner, but the store was vacant now. Franklin Lamb, who was his supervisor, and opened and closed the store around his job at the Food Co-op, told him that a famous painter used to live across the street until he went off to play baseball in Mexico.

"Watch your cash drawer," he said to John Lamb. "And if anyone asks for something, write it down. We can see about getting it for them and it helps to build our mailing list."

"I will."

"*Ba-Abba*," said Franklin and he went off to his day of making organic sandwich spreads.

"*Ba-Abba*," answered William Goodwin.

Scott Lamb had given him lots to read and he was only one–third through *The Gift of the Tau*. However, John Lamb made sure to keep alert for customers and even shoplifters, who he was told occasionally made their way over from Germantown. If they came into the store, he would be able to tell from the time he spent incarcerated. That seemed like long ago, and now, at the same time.

William Goodwin read from his book and said his prayers. There were three telephone calls, one inquiring if they had anything by "Farrell and the Flames," a wrong number, and Franklin, asking if everything was okay and would he like faux chicken salad on multi-grain bread for lunch, which he was happy to have.

A customer came in at eleven o'clock. "You're new here," he said.

"Yes, I am."

"Do you have Phil Ochs' *Bwatue*?"

William Goodwin came from behind the counter and started looking through the "O's"

"You won't have it. Anything by The Sundowners? Jim Glover? I don't think so," the customer said. "Nothing will be the same since Richie Havens died."

At noon, Franklin Lamb came over and brought the sandwich and a cranberry spritzer. "Any business?" he asked.

"A phone call for Farrell and the Flames and at eleven o'clock somebody who said he only wanted what we don't have."

"That's okay. Most of the sales are through the website, but we have to have a place for the inventory and this is a way to be a good neighbor."

At five o'clock, they closed the store together and walked back to their communal home. On the way, Franklin talked about the time he spent in the Navy and India and that he would present tonight after dinner, so that he was going to walk on a bit to prepare. He took some notes from his back pocket and began studying them while he walked.

Edmund Brodeur returned at seven o'clock that evening from checking on the arrangements for the fishing trip. Scott Lamb told him that Anna and Ariel were not going because of the vaccination, which was very much against his wishes.

"Your wife is right, Scott. I am glad you agreed. We must keep our children safe. Give her some willow root if her temperature goes about 100° and don't worry. "*Ba-Abba.*"

The household awoke at 4:30 on the day of the trip to the Chesapeake. They would breakfast on the yellow school bus after morning prayer. In the back of the bus were insulated bags for each of the fishermen.

"The Captain will provide us with rods and reels or hand-lines if you prefer. Just remember to lower your bags into the ocean by the strings attached to keep them cool," said Edmund Brodeur. "We have ginger root if you are feeling sick. Also remember the Shiatsu points on your wrists, although that is rarely necessary for we who do not eat flesh. I will be driving ahead to check on the arrangements," said Oleg Kutzenov. "It's a beautiful day."

He circled back to the communal home on Wayne Avenue where Anna and Ariel stayed behind. The child was fussing, so he did not interrupt Anna while she was comforting her baby. When the child had nursed herself to sleep, Oleg Kutzenov slit their throats.

CHAPTER TWELVE

Carrington drove the white limo like he knew how to, which was staying in the right lane and not trying to be a cowboy.

There was no trouble at all until about Exit 8 where it narrowed from three lanes. A blue Beamer, the 500 series, cut them out and Carrington had to show he could handle the limousine.

"Is everything alright?" said Grace.

"Everything's okay, Ms. Savoy," said the driver.

"In a pig's eye it is," Rook said. "Cool it."

The traffic backed up a mile ahead and they crept along for another fifteen minutes until it thinned out. A statie had pulled the BMW over right before the ramp to the Pennsylvania connector at Exit 6 and was swinging back into traffic.

"Philly's loss," said Rook.

"Or Camden's," said Carrington. "Garden spot of the world."

"I had fried chicken there," said Gracie "And pizza, actually fried chicken pizza. Delish. But they left the bone in. 'That's what she said'. Pascetta's the place was called. A fast guy named Bobby took me there. He knew all the good pizza places in the world. He said Trenton had the best."

"Are you getting hungry, Ms. Savoy?" asked Carrington.

She lit a cigarette and cracked the window.

"I'm fine. But if we pass anything interesting, let me know. I want to pretend I can see it. But would you give a thirsty girl a drinky-poo of whatever pedestrian white wine Jake stocked."

Lucas was pouring her drink when the Beamer came up again, doing eighty, eighty-five.

"Watch him," Rook said.

Duane Carrington reached under the seat and brought out a Remington 9 mili.

"That's not smart," Rook told him.

"Just doing my job like the Judge told me to."

Lucas leaned forward. "You want to get pinched that's on you. You're going to get Ms. Savoy hurt, that's on me. Pull over."

"Yay!" said Grace. "Here, hold my drink so I can clap. Two big men fighting over me."

"Pull over and let the BMW go," Rook said. "And give me your weapon so nobody gets hurt."

"I can handle this," the driver said.

Lucas put his hand on the driver's shoulder. "And I'm not asking."

"Don't touch me. Don't ever touch me," Carrington said. But he did what he was told.

"Boys, boys," said Grace Savoy. "Enough already. I'm going to get frown lines, which I won't like at all. Kenneth, whatever you were doing to upset Mr. Rook, stop it, or I'll tell Jake. Lucas, you be a good boy, too."

Nice. Now your client's got you playing in the sandbox.

"Next time, I'm driving, Grace. No doubt I'm doing that or somebody else is doing your PP," said Lucas.

"There is no somebody else, though Kenny you are a good boy, too. But you shouldn't have said PP. Now I have to go potty. I really do."

"There's a rest stop up ahead on the other side," said Rook.

Carrington touched the bill of his chauffeur's cap. "Yes, sir," he said.

"What's it called?" said Grace. "The place we're stopping at so I can pee? In New Jersey they all have names, right? Clara Barton, the nurse. Joyce Kilmer, who was a man. James Fennimore Cooper, I think I sat in his lap once."

"Isn't he dead, Ms. Savoy?"

"Why he is, Duane. Correct. I was at Cooperstown, The Hall of Fame. A big stone lap, but that was before he made my favorite movie."

"*The Last of the Mohicans*," Judge Schwarzman told me to play it if you get bored," said Carrington.

"'I will find you', How romantic. Daniel Day Lewis. Or was it Doris Day or Jerry Lewis?" said Grace Savoy.

The driver began his detour and pulled into the service area. "I'll stop at the curb," he said.

"I'll take Ms. Savoy in," said Rook. "Then I'll watch the car if you need."

Grace grabbed Rook's arm as he helped her out of the limo. "Be still my heart," she said. "Popeye's. I can smell it. You order for me." Then she stopped and lit another cigarette. "No, no. I'll not be tempted. Nothing shall make me betray Roy Rogers."

Lucas waited until she was done her smoke, then walked her inside and over to the ladies room.

"Five minutes," he said.

"And if I linger?"

"I'll come in after you," Rook told her.

"Guns blazing?"

"Five minutes, Gracie. And try to unwind."

"Cup of coffee will do that, Lucas boy. And get yourself one and one for Duane. He's such a dear."

"I'll wait until you come out."

Grace Savoy was back out of the restroom in exactly five minutes. "It was a game we played at the Wade School for the Blind. I can tell exactly how much time has expired. Wake me up in the middle of the night, and I know exactly what time it is. See, forty-five seconds passed since I pretended to wash my hands."

"You want something?" Rook asked.

"Take me back out to the car, Lucas instead of the coffee. The smell of the chicken and biscuits is making me insane."

"Is that what it is?"

"Don't be cross with me," she said. "Whatever that means. I think it means 'pissed-off'. Now I do want a latte´ or something like that."

They went back out to the car, then Carrington went in and got her coffee and when he came back out, he and Grace leaned against the vehicle, drinking their coffee and smoking. Rook walked around to the other side of the limo so he wasn't breathing in the second-hand smoke, which if you've already been shot in the chest and had your heart worked on, you try to avoid, the fumes off the highway being bad enough.

The ride went smooth until the usual back up at I-95. Then they were on their way to the location. Grace Savoy was even quiet for an hour or so while she fell asleep.

Carrington did all right, although he missed the 495 cut-off near Wilmington, which meant they picked up more traffic. When Grace woke up, she knew exactly how much time had gone by and how much more to go until they reached the Roy Rogers at the Maryland House service area.

"Please press on, Duane. I do not wish to keep my holster of fries waiting."

"Will do," he said, again touching the imaginary brim of the chauffeur's hat that was on the seat next to him.

Brodeur's flock was happily riding to their day's outing and their own death. The school bus made slow time from New Jersey south. The family of The Tau, all known as Lamb, sang songs, and ate their snacks of organic this and home grown that, unaware that they would be forever known as terrorist murderers, as they were that Anna and her baby had been slaughtered.

Once the Tau was into Maryland, the bus driver announced that they were stopping at the rest stop to stretch their legs and freshen up there. Lucas Rook was paying a visit to the Men's Room at the same rest area while Carrington and Gracie were enjoying their feast of fried chicken and French fries.

When William Goodwin came into the lavatory, Rook slammed his face against the wall and then down against the urinal. By the time anyone could respond, Lucas was back outside and then miles down I-95 in the white limousine.

CHAPTER THIRTEEN

It was Oleg Kutzenov's intention to be a thousand miles away when Dr. Mauritani's genius caused the huge explosion in the Chesapeake Bay and the resultant tsunami rushing towards Washington. He also knew that it was possible that something would go amiss. Hadn't there been the failure of Aum Shinrikyo to complete their True Lamb of God's cyanide attack in the Tokyo subway system? Hadn't a simple mechanical malfunction derailed that attempt to kill tens of thousands? And had not he and Marat Belov failed in his attempt to free their Messiah, Shoko Ashara, from his black iron prison?

He was therefore unhappy, but not unprepared, when he heard Scott Lamb's phone message that there had been an incident at the Maryland House rest stop and that they were going to be delayed. John Lamb had been injured and the state police were interviewing him and had sent for an ambulance, although his injuries did not seem life threatening.

Scott also related that he had called the captain of the Aunt Isabel to say that they were going to be late, but would not expect a discount. He then called his wife at the Tau home to share with her, but there was no answer.

As an experienced operative, Edmund Brodeur had made provisions for possible delay or even the necessity of canceling the operation. The presence and purchase of the HMX explosives, which were hidden in the bottom of the boat, were not traceable to him, Dr. Mauritani, Marat Belov, or the Foundation. The Tau only, was at risk and they were disposable.

The alternatives now were not optimal, but acceptable. If the Aunt Isabel waited for its passengers, the two explosions, the first to sink the boat and the second to cause the tidal wave, would only cause the tsunami if the optimal depth of water had been reached. It was also possible that the boat might explode at dockside or not at the desired location and with strangers aboard. There also always was the possibility, that the explosives would be discovered.

In each of the circumstances, the news media would soon enough be deluging their audience with pictures and information of the Tau, Aum Shinrikyo, and their Lamb of God, Shoko Ashara. All their actions in the past would be brought to life again, and they would be blamed for the death of the woman and child who were slain in the house on Wayne Avenue.

Kutzenov's greatest concern was the disappointment of Marat Belov and The Foundation. This could have most deadly consequences. He called Reba Nemerov on her cel phone.

"It's raining here," he said.

"You must have the wrong number," she answered.

It took about five minutes for the Maryland State Police to find out that the victim of the restroom beating was a celebrity.

"My name is William Goodwin," he said through the ice pack he held on his face.

The trooper turned to Franklin Lamb. "So his name is not 'John Lamb' like you just told me."

"Lamb is our family. We're all one family," Franklin said, touching the symbol of the Tau he wore around his neck.

"So he could be anybody, is what you're telling me?"

"We are one in The Messiah's Love."

"Terrific, Mr. Lamb. Why don't you and the rest of your 'family' take a seat on your bus? I'll have a little chat with John, William, whatever."

The trooper walked Goodwin over to his unmarked Camaro and opened the back door.

"Am I under arrest?" Goodwin asked.

"For sure if you bleed on my upholstery here. Meanwhile, I'm going to run you for wants and warrants. You come up clean, you can go picnic with your church group."

"We are one in The One True Lamb of God," said Goodwin. Only we can bring salvation from the coming doom of 2012."

"Right. Now meantime, you just keep quiet until I tell you different."

Nothing local or state came up, but Goodwin's babbling about his being beaten before for no reason, led to his talking about his incarceration and then his conviction for involuntary manslaughter. Another fifteen minutes and a second cruiser pulled up with Lieutenant Gingold, a big man with a square face.

"I didn't do anything wrong," said William Goodwin. "It was the drug company."

"You got what you deserved no matter what your slick lawyers say. Get on that bus. Don't stop until you're out of my state. You understand me? " said the Lieutenant.

"Yes, yes."

"Yes, what?" said Lieutenant Gingold.

"Yes, sir, I mean…"

The trooper leaned in. "They're going to the Chesapeake, LT. Some kind of religious group, to do some fishing."

"Yes," said Goodwin with his eyes looking down at the ground.

"You go have your day trip with your friends, who probably don't know what you are, do they?" said Lieutenant Gingold. "Meanwhile, I'm going to call down to my barracks at Sunderland to let them know you are coming. Kind of like my own Megan's Law."

"And the person who beat me, did this to me?" asked John Lamb.

"We'll look into that. Now you have a nice day and don't get too much sun. Terrible for your skin. Absolutely terrible."

Victoria, who had been a nurse in her earlier life, came over and saw to John.

"What they said…" he started.

"We are all born again in the Tau," said Victoria Lamb. "Purified by the love of our Father, the Blind Messiah. Now go clean off the dried blood and I'll pack your nose for you," she told Goodwin. "And you're going to need some dental work, I'm afraid. Your front two teeth are broken in half."

William nodded. "They're just crowns. It happened before."

Victoria Lamb got the supervisor from Starbucks to give her some ice. She sat with John Lamb when they got on the bus and put her hand on his.

"We are a family," she said.

William Goodwin sat motionless, and then turned away so that she would not see him cry. The tears came easily for what had just happened to him, his trial and conviction, and the death of his son, and his guilt, all-becoming one within him, so soon he was shaking with it.

Victoria leaned in. "Try not to breathe through your nose," she said. "The clotting will break up," which sounded silly to him, and he began to laugh, first one, then the other, the laughter, the crying, with Victoria's hand on his.

There was meditation and the prayers before lunch led by Scott Lamb, who still had not been able to reach his Anna. The Tau ate the lunches that they had prepared, goat cheese and sprouts on oatmeal bread and some organic carrots they had grown, and for dessert, some apple slices with cinnamon.

They could smell the water of the Chesapeake as they drew near and they put the windows down so they could enjoy it, and the sound of the gulls circling overhead and the sight of the other water birds.

Victoria Lamb squeezed William's hand. "What a glorious day it will be," she said.

The Tau parked their bus at the marina and walked towards the sign, "Aunt Isabel," When they got there, the boat was gone.

"Couldn't wait," said the deckhand on the Bridget Grey, which was still taking on fisherman. "Your captain asked for me to take you out if you want. He said he couldn't wait."

CHAPTER FOURTEEN

Grace Savoy ate her fried chicken and fries with a pair of rubber gloves on.

"You don't know how the tiniest spot of dead cluck-cluck grease can ruin an otherwise perfect portrait," she said.

"I hear you," added the driver, his mouth filled with drumstick and biscuit. "Myself, I've got to be careful to use a couple of those wet-knaps to wipe the steering wheel down or my ass is grass."

"Is that a fact?" said Lucas Rook.

"Speaking of which," said Gracie as she tossed a joint into the front seat.

"No you don't," Rook said. "No smoking, holding or transporting. Hand it over, Duane. You, too, Grace. And I mean it."

"I'm just the hired help," said Carrington.

"And I'm the big bad wolf," Lucas told him.

The driver handed the joint to Rook who split the paper and let its contents out of the window.

"You'll have to search me," said Grace Savoy. I'd love that, too."

"No, I won't, Gracie. I'll just have to let myself out. Pull over."

"I can do this, Ms. Savoy," said Duane. "Like you know, I take the Judge all around."

"Oh, drat," said the supermodel as she handed over two marijuana cigarettes.

"The rest of it," said Rook.

"I gave you all I was holding, Lucas. Except the rest which is in my cootchie."

"Pull over, Duane."

Carrington didn't.

Rook leaned forward. "I said, pull over."

"I work for Ms. Savoy and Judge Schwarzman," he said, switching into the passing lane.

Rook brought his slapjack out.

"We're about to have a situation here," he said.

"Problema?" asked Grace.

"Big problema. Which is going to be settled one way or another, neither of which is going to help you with your fashion job or Duane with his left collar bone."

"Carrington, do as he said."

"Because she said so," said the driver.

"Terrific. I'm impressed. Just pull over," Rook said.

Carrington swung back into the right lane and onto the shoulder.

"Okay, kids. Either one of you is holding anything illegal, and I mean anything, you give it up right now. I'm not going upside down in a ditch or taking a pinch."

"All I got is one more blunt in my bag. No, two," said Gracie.

"Field strip them, split the paper, and lose the dope. Now."

Grace Savoy did as she was told and popped a pill. "That was a Valium, five milligrams. Doctor's orders. This is so upsetting."

"And?"

"I've got Lorazepam and some other thing I don't know what it is. But they're all prescribed."

"Anything else?"

"Birth control pills. See, I'm still fertile as a turtle. Flintstone vitamins, the chewy kind, and some Tic-tacs, the orange kind."

"Carrington?" asked Lucas.

"I'm clean."

"Okay, people, let's get back on the road," Rook told them.

Duane Carrington handled the rest of the run into The Capital without an issue and kept his mouth shut until they reached the National Mall.

"Safe and sound, Ms. Savoy," he said.

"Thank you, gentlemen. You see a little faggy-type trying to look like he knows what he's doing, tell me," she said.

"More trouble from Lawrence again?" asked Rook.

"Everybody will just have to get along. Honest Abe would insist." She cracked her window and lit a cigarette. "He's at Daniel French Drive, as a matter of fact."

Carrington pulled as close as he could.

"Or maybe at the Reflecting Pool. I wonder if my reflection's blind, too." Gracie took her last hit of menthol and nicotine and flicked her cigarette out the window. "Lucas, dear, you know what Lawrence looks like. Would you be a dear and go find him?"

A park ranger came over and knocked on the driver's window. "We've a very strict no littering policy," he said. "And there's no stopping here."

Grace opened her tinted window and showed the ranger her beautiful face. "I'm blind, "she said. "Absolutely one hundred percent."

"I'm sorry, ma'am, but please do as I ask."

Rook got out. "I'll go get Larry. Duane can get the cigarette butt and then we'll meet back here."

"Or the Reflecting Pool," said Carrington.

"Would you like my autograph?" said Grace Savoy.

"I'm fine, ma'am. Thank you for your cooperation."

"We'll be shooting a commercial. You're welcome to watch. Or even be in it. Isn't that right?"

Lucas had already started after Grace's director. This would be the third time they'd be on the same shoot and no doubt, it would be just as annoying.

"Isn't that right, whichever or both of my hired hands is still here?" asked Grace again.

"That's right," said Duane.

"Now don't forget that ciggy butt, dear," she told him.

Lucas Rook found Larry behind one of the forty-four feet columns at the entrance.

"Just you?" said Lucas.

"Which was fine until a second ago."

"Where are your people?" asked Rook. "The hangers-on, some co-ed or two, who can't resist your round eyeglasses and that thing you wear, a 'dickey', right?"

"It's an ascot, as if that mattered to you in the slightest." He took a Gauliose from his cigarette case. "Is Ms. Savoy with you?"

Lucas pretended to search his pockets.

"Must we go through this ridiculous behavior again?"

"Not necessarily. I could always do what I want to do which is kicking your ass, but then I might not get paid."

Lawrence played with his French cigarette. "You don't like me very much, do you?"

"Don't have to," said Lucas. "Just doing my job, which right now is Ms. Savoy said for me to find you."

"You did that. Now please tell her I'll be inside in the south chamber. It's where the Gettysburg Address is."

"I'm supposed to bring you," Rook told him.

"That isn't at all appropriate, but I know how she can be. Give me twenty minutes."

"You can catch your smoke on the way, Larry. We're going".

The supermodel in the back of the white limousine was holding a pair of instant ice packs to her face as Rook brought her director over.

"Have you walked through the location?" Lawrence asked her.

She opened the blacked-out window.

"Absolutely. It's just what I remembered it to be. Stunning, perfect, which is how I look," she said and she removed the ice.

"Nothing today. Tomorrow morning at five-thirty. Please no drinking tonight."

"I'll be staying at The Willard," she answered. "Now Mr. Bodyguard, Jeeves, my chariot, please."

Rook got in and Duane drove them away.

"It's such crap," said Gracie as she lit another Kool. "I'm supposed to do a walk-through, pick-up the vibe. It's all the same to me. I might just as well be sitting on Santa's lap in Macy's window." She took a deep drag on her smoke and spoke as she exhaled,

"In this temple
As in the Hearts of the People
For whom he saved the Union
The Memory of Abraham Lincoln
Is enshrined forever."

"I learned that in school for extra credit. Duane Carrington. Would you recite the Gettysburg Address for us?"

"I got to keep my mind on my driving, Ms. Grace."

Lucas knew from what Sid Rosen had told him that there was a mistake in the carving of one of Lincoln's lines, but kept it to himself.

They went to the hotel.

"I have two rooms, per my contract," said Grace. And Jake has one for the two of us, so you two won't have to be bunkies."

"I'll stay outside of your door, Gracie." said Rook.

"But won't that stifle the Judge? I can't have that. He's a moaner, you know."

"Way too much information, Grace. And I have a job to do. Let me see the lay-out and talk to hotel security before I make you any promises."

Jack Keith, a sergeant with the Miami PD before becoming the Head of Security at the Willard, gave Lucas what he needed. "We have VIP's all the time, diplomats and the like, so I run a pretty tight ship. Not to mention we got every kind of surveillance toy you could think of."

"Appreciate that," said Rook. "I got me one of those cover girl models and a retired Judge."

"Right, and you got two rooms on the floor down the hall."

"I need to have a gig like yours," Lucas said. "This bodyguard work's a pain in my New York ass."

"I hear you. You want access to the interior surveillance?"

"I don't think he would like that. Me neither. They'll likely be pretty active in the sack. What would be good is the old standby chair outside the room, or the end of the hall at least."

"Can't do. Spook the clientele. I'll ramp up the security, like they're royalty. They'll be safe as a bug in a rug, which we don't have here anyways, bedbugs, I mean. Also, I'll let my people know you're here. The driver, he okay?"

"The driver wishes he was more."

"We're good then." Keith handed over his card and wrote his cel on it. "Anything doesn't go smooth as silk, you let me know."

The night went easy, even though The Swan being there, meant another thing altogether. The next morning, the union boys and the park rangers both gave Lawrence a raft of shit, which was a good thing, not only because he was a sawed-off sissy prick, but it also meant lots of OT. Otherwise, the job moved okay. Grace Savoy looked like magic.

Afterwards, Jake Schwarzman rode with Gracie and Rook on the way back to New York. Mostly he talked on the phone, and they stopped again for fried chicken like she wanted to.

CHAPTER FIFTEEN

When Lucas Rook got back to his place at the Saint Claire, there were messages on his house and business line. Texts were a waste because you couldn't hear what they were saying other than the words. Plus like e-mails, they were there forever, which made things backwards, phone-buying wise. Also, you see two, three people walking down the street they're on their gizmos, which is a perfect invitation for somebody to snatch their stuff or jack them.

There was a return call from Attorney Maidman that he had a client who needs a little skiptracing work, which means either the lawyer can't find the shitbird by the computer, or there's some confidentiality issues he doesn't want to get involved in. He also had some transom work. Domestic jobs you usually pass on, because even though the subject's usually a real loser, maybe he doesn't like seeing you as part of his life going down the toilet and things get rougher than you're getting paid for.

Lucas called Catherine Wren back last.

"Remember the bookstore that closed, Ross'? You were there with me last year," she said.

"They served wine and cheese. And veggies. You know how much I love that." Lucas arched his back to stretch out his chest muscles from where he had been shot.

"I know you're joking with me now," Catherine said. "Ross and his wife moved back and have a baby now. We're having a kind of belated shower for them at Miguel's,

"They have any cheese and beans there? Maybe a little rice?"

"You liked the food at Miguel's. Plus you can have flan for dessert. In bed."

"What more could a man ask for? What time?"

"Dinner's at eight."

"I'll be at your place at seven," Lucas told her and he hung up.

He had time to get a decent workout by doing the fire stairs. In the old days, he could have run it, but his leg and taking three in the chest from Dwight Graves, meant fast walking, which you pretend is running.

Grace Savoy stuck her head out of her place as he came into their hallway.

"It's Rook, Gracie."

"I can tell," she answered. "You should know after all this time. We have to go back to re-shoot Honest

Abe. He was not gay as some people say. I know. I sat on his lap."

"Going out of town, Gracie."

Grace Savoy walked over to him. "You smell so salty," she said. "Like Genoa salami actually."

"Actually, I'm going to shower off this salami smell and head out, Grace. I've got other clients. I just can't pick up and go. Carrington could drive and I'll get you somebody good for security."

"I mean tomorrow morning. The crack of dawn. I get paid double, and so will you. In and out. 'That's what she said.' The kids say that. Plus, if I use somebody else, maybe I'll want them to protect me the next time."

"Got to get mileage, too, Grace. We can take Sid's Towne Car."

"Deal," she said. "See you".

Lucas showered and changed so he could get through the Holland Tunnel before it became a mess. He called Catherine from the Jersey Turnpike that he'd be early, which maybe would count against not staying over or leaving when it was still dark to make Grace Savoy's job. One of these days, he's going to get a couple of decent corporate clients again, like the funeral company and Best Buy were, and then he wouldn't have to be living like a gypsy.

Lucas got Catherine Wren's machine at home and her cel was off. If he didn't see her when he got to the campus, he'd hang around and scare the Princeton kids. He saw her walking toward her building after about twenty minutes of playing Narco.

"What a nice surprise. It's been a dismal day so far." She kissed him on the cheek.

"Your kids have trouble with Spenser again. Hawk's a difficult character to fathom." A good word he picked up along the way.

She smiled.

"Actually, even here the students have trouble reading anything unless it's not on their phone anymore." She squeezed his arm. "You're early. What a nice surprise. Would you like to get a cup of coffee?"

"At your place, Cat."

He walked her to her car and followed her back to her little house with the honeysuckles outside. They made love in her soft bed and after, she read verses to him from somebody who he didn't exactly understand, but the words sounded like music.

They went to Miguel's early so that they could have real dinner before the reception for The Rutledges in the room off to the left. Catherine did the ordering except for the beer, and they joked about how he thought mole' was going to be a rodent. Good coffee and flan to go for dessert as the old customers of the bookstore started to show up.

Ross and his wife had moved away when the book business collapsed. But now that they had a kid, they were back, thanks to Catherine and a group of her friends finding him a job in The Firestone Library on campus

Catherine hugged Ross and he shook Rook's hand. "Mrs. R's at home with little Ross," he said. "Comet here's my date. Getting a little gray, this golden retriever of ours, but he's still the best."

It was a good thing they had eaten dinner, because what they served at the reception wouldn't have kept a bird alive. There was a lot of talk about books and what was going to happen to them, and this guy Gutenberg, who probably was turning over in his grave. Some of the group wanted to go back to somebody's house, which meant smoking dope and talking politics, neither of which were going to do him and Cat's evening any good.

"Grace Savoy asked me," Rook said in the hall, "that I take her down to D.C. tomorrow to redo some of their shots."

"You won't be staying with me tonight?"

"I am, but I'll have to leave real early."

"I understand," said Catherine. "Let me say my goodbyes and then we'll go home."

Catherine made a good cup of coffee back at her place with the Gaggia coffee maker he had gotten for her for Christmas. Then they went to bed. Before she turned the light out, she kissed each of the scars from the three bullet holes in his chest and where Doc Buechner in the ER and then Di Bona, the cardiologist, had cut him open to save his life.

Lucas had to leave in the middle of the night to get back to the City. Catherine walked him to the door. "We're very lucky," she said. "You know that, Lucas Rook. I know you do."

The run back to Manhattan was easy and when Rook dropped his brother's Avanti at Rosen's garage, Sid was waiting for him and had the Towne Car up front.

"You know a guy named, Gutenberg?" said Rook. "I was at what they call a 'wine and cheese'. Big topic of conversation."

"One 'T' or two?" asked the garageman. "One, you're talking Johannes Gutenberg, who invented the movable type printing press, which he said came to him like a 'ray of light'. That was a good thing because before that, he was involved in some scam selling polished mirrors to pilgrims to capture 'the holy light'." He underhanded the car keys. "Two, you're talking, Steve, a Brooklyn Boy. *Police Academy*, you must have loved that. *Cocoon*. Actually started as a messenger, no credit in the 1977 stinker, *Roller Coaster*. The poor bastard was eliminated from DWTS in 2008."

"Whatever that is, Sidney. I'm taking Grace Savoy to D.C. so the usual add-on because there's no way she's not going to smoke."

"Agreed to, and have a safe trip, compadre," said Sidney. "Now let me piss for the twelfth time this evening."

Rook swung the vehicle over to his place. He called Grace on the way over, but it rang and rang, which meant she was in the shower, or there was something wrong. He gave the doorman a twenty to drive the Towne Car around the block until he came down and then went upstairs to their floor. There was an envelope pinned to his door. A check for two-fifty inside and a note that she had another fight with Lawrence and the shoot was off. "A thousand sorries," and that she was at Jake's.

Rook drove back to Sid Rosen's and they went out for ham and eggs at Kroner's. Then he went to sleep. His cel rang at nine o'clock. It was Philadelphia lawyer extraordinaire, Warren G. Phelps, who had a job for him.

CHAPTER SIXTEEN

Edmund Brodeur knew that Toronto was close enough that a member of The Foundation could arrive and hold a personal debriefing in a matter of hours. Such was important, not only to serve the needs of his employer, but also to show that he did not fear that the failure of the operation made him a target of Marat Belov. Were that actually the case, his life expectancy would be brief.

It was as easy for Oleg Kutzenov to change from Brodeur, as it was to become someone else. The Marriott on Bay Street was convenient and the Foundation's emissary, Reba Nemerov, arrived as he was eating an early dinner. "Nicole Meunier," she said, putting down her briefcase and extending her hand.

He let the reference to the captain of the French Hockey team pass. "Stefan Beltz," he said, shaking hands most briefly. Kutzenov gestured for the waiter.

"Just coffee," said Reba.

"It is a pleasure to meet with you," he told her.

"And you as well, Mr. Beltz. How is business, as the Americans say?"

Her coffee arrived. Kutzenov gestured that he did not wish his refilled.

"I am waiting for an addition to my product line."

She lifted her cup, and then put it down. "I understand, Mr. Beltz. Or perhaps an expansion of your territory."

"That is not up to me, Ms. Meunier. I am one who follows directions."

"Which must be difficult in this contracting economy. We believe that it is prudent to attend to our existing clientele, which is to say that continued distractive market activity is not prudent."

"I understand. That is a wise philosophy," said Oleg Kutzenov. "Would you like a croissant, perhaps?"

Nemerov stood up. "I'm afraid not. I do have another meeting."

They shook hands again and she left. Beltz called for the waiter to order dessert as a demonstration that he had little else on his mind. After he had finished his cake and a second cup of coffee, he returned to his room and prepared to leave.

The message the Foundation had sent him was clear. His prime responsibility was that he leave no un-neutralized threats or exposure. Only then, was he to return to his initial assignment. The words spoken by Reba Nemerov were his directions and a warning.

Rather than avoid The Tau and the Philadelphia murder scene, which as likely as not The Foundation now knew about, he would return to Philadelphia and contain it.

Stefan Beltz took the two and a half hour train ride to Quebec and from there a New York flight from Lessage Airport. As Edmund Brodeur, he rode Amtrak to Philadelphia and then a taxi to the house on Wayne Avenue. There was a white police cruiser parked across the street and remnants of yellow crime scene tape on the front door.

Victoria Lamb met him at the front door. "Blessed be the One True Messiah," she said, but her eyes looked like empty windows.

"What happened?" Brodeur asked.

Victoria stepped outside, covering her face with her hands. "Someone killed Anna and the baby. Our only baby in this house."

"Do you need to sit down? I'll pray with you," he said.

"Franklin has directed us all to be taking St. John's Wart for our nerves, which was before the detectives came for John Lamb. He is back now." She started to cry, quietly first, then almost a wail.

Oleg Kutzenov put his arm around Victoria Lamb and helped her inside.

She took deep breaths. "There were police here. There was blood everywhere," she said. "We're supposed to tell you to call Detective Moore when you come in. His card is on the bulletin board in the meeting room."

"I'll ask our One True Messiah to bring you, and all of those who are suffering, His blessing and strength."

"Yes, yes," she said. "Particularly, for Scott Lamb."

"Of course, my child. *Ba-Abba*. Father is coming."

"And John Lamb. It's been so hard for him, getting beaten by a perfect stranger he didn't even see and then what happened here."

"Did he share with you?" asked Kutzenov.

"John said that after evening prayers he would share with us, but when he came back from seeing his lawyer, which he said we all should have, particularly we innocents, he told me that he would not be sharing after prayer."

"All prayers of we who are the Tau, the Last who shall be the First, are sharing, Victoria. Come sit down and after I have tended to Scott, we shall pray together."

Scott Lamb was in his room, pale and almost catatonic.

"May the blessings of the True Lamb of God, bring you comfort," said Edmund Brodeur.

"They're gone. Someone killed them. Killed them. There was so much blood on the floor. So much." He covered his face with his hands. "My little girl. My Anna."

"Our Father has taken them to his bosom," Brodeur answered.

The childless widower was silent and did not move. Then his mouth moved to speak, but no words came out.

Victoria came to the doorway. "There's a man downstairs. He's a detective and he's here to see John."

"What did he say?" asked Brodeur.

"First, he asked for William someone. Then John."

"Is John coming down?"

"He is. May we have that tea now?" asked Victoria.

Oleg Kutzenov walked her into the kitchen, where he stood so he could see the rough looking man in the leather jacket now inside their house.

When Goodwin saw who it was, he started back up the steps.

"It's okay, Bill." Rook told him. "Your lawyer, Warren Phelps, sent me. You called Judge Schwarzman, who told you to call Warren. The Judge also wants to know you're alright and that Attorney Phelps and he will be working together."

John Lamb looked over at Brodeur, who nodded it was all right.

"We can go into the yard," said Brodeur.

"Me and my client," said Lucas. "Let's do it like that."

"I thought you didn't believe me," William Goodwin told Rook when they were outside.

"I work for the lawyers."

"How do I know Judge Schwarzman's…?"

"Working with Warren Phelps, William? Because I wouldn't make that up and you can call them both."

"I thought that you were going to beat me next time you saw me?"

"We're okay there. What's not okay is the Philly PD, which I know is going to be all over you for the murders."

"I didn't do it. Do you believe me?"

"On this I do. You want to know why?"

William Goodwin nodded.

"Too much blood. You're not the type. What you are is somebody who shouldn't be talking to anybody but your lawyers and me. You understand?"

"I do, but the police already came for me. I called Judge Schwarzman. They let me leave when a lawyer from Mr. Phelps' office showed up. I have his card upstairs. He dressed like Matlock and had red hair."

"Did you tell them who you are, give them your real name?"

William Goodwin nodded. "I had to."

"Like your attorney said, I'm sure, and I just told you, you don't say anything to anybody. That means nobody. The police talk to you again, you tell them Warren Phelps is your attorney. Anybody here is curious, whatever, you say zero, nothing. You want out of here or need anything, you call me on my cel. You understand a hundred percent?"

Rook gave John Lamb his card with the chess piece on it and two cards from Warren Phelps. Then he left.

Oleg Kutzenov did not wait before seeing to William Goodwin. "Awful things have happened here, John," he said. "But our family and the Love of our true Messiah shall see us through."

He put his hand on John Lamb's shoulder, but Goodwin pulled away.

"I am sorry," said Brodeur. "I shall send you my comfort and that of our Father with my mind and heart. Have you taken your herbs? They will calm you as well. And that policeman, who was just here, should not come back. It is upsetting to all our family."

"He works for my lawyer," said Goodwin touching the wooden Tau he wore around his neck. "He is very powerful, my lawyer is. He said I must not speak to anyone. And Mr. Rook was a gold shield detective in New York. He'll find who killed Anna and her child and he will protect us."

"That's good, John Lamb, very good. Remember, I am here for you. I shall pray for you to Our One True Savior, Shoko Ashara. And if you need me, everything that you tell me is protected, privileged."

Brodeur turned to leave, then back again. "Your lawyer's and investigator's phone numbers, I should have them just in case."

William Goodwin gave him one of the Warren Phelps' cards and showed him Rook's.

"Our Father will take care of you, John Lamb. And I am his servant. I hope that it is a comfort. Everything will work out."

Then Oleg Kutzenov retired to his room. William Goodwin would be a perfect explanation for the killings. Then the meeting with Dr. Mauritani. And all would be well.

CHAPTER SEVENTEEN

The last time Lucas Rook was in Philly, it was the Delbert Fine case. That tattooed freak got what was coming to him, but not before he killed Detective Jimmy Salerno and cut off the head of Janet Shay, who was on those television shows for kids in the '60's. This time down, he was going to let the Philly PD do the heavy lifting.

What it was going to be was good old-fashioned private detective business, for which you're getting good money for it. And somebody else is going to do the dirty work. First thing, is to find out who's around. Let them know you're hired and that you're not going to be stepping on anybody's brogans. Anything you come up with, you'll give to the catching detectives and try to stay out of their way.

What you already know is that the City of Brotherly Love still got lots of crime, despite Seth Williams, the DA, who's the real deal. One weekend, twenty-six shootings. Still over three hundred murders every year. The latest, they call it a "flash mob", which is maybe a hundred kids of the African American persuasion, jump somebody in a suit and beat the shit out of him. The felons-in-training need sports programs and computers, the social workers say. What they need is a serious beat-down, all of them, after which you dump them all across the river in Camden. Let the wildlife take care of each other.

You make your calls and find out Inspector Zinn finally put his papers in. Captain Cisone moved up a slot. Sam Nessel, the dwarf, is still the ME. You try Inspector Cisone, but he's not in. Then you go over to Bill Higgins' place, which isn't a cop's hangout any more, but trying to be an Italian restaurant.

The clock in your stomach goes off like the alligator in *Peter Pan,* so you answer back with your expense account, a veal parm sandwich with a couple of light beers, the joint not having Yuengling, which is odd, since Philly's in Pennsylvania where the brew's from.

Then, it's over to Northwest Detectives where Big Joe Garrett's not working the desk anymore, so that you got to take out your PI license and jump through some hoops until Lieutenant Esposito's coming down the steps, looking as hot as ever, but still with "boss" written all over her.

"Look what the cat dragged in," she said. "He's with me," she told the desk.

"I wish," Lucas said.

"I know you do. Walk with me," which like he figured, meant she was going to catch a smoke.

"Working for Warren Phelps on that Wayne Avenue double," he told her.

"Fancy, Warren Phelps." She lit-up.

"His creepo client didn't do it," said Rook.

"They never do. FYI, Doc Nessel is working up the preliminary e-val."

Lucas nodded in appreciation.

"That sawed off character still around?"

"Sam had some accounting issues, but no way if you're one of the little people, they get rid of you. You going out to interview Sam, I'll call ahead."

"Appreciate it."

"Hawkey and Lefkoe got the job," she said as she turned her head to exhale a stream of smoke.

Lucas popped one of the mints he took compliments of Esposito. "The cowboy and Gene, Gene the Dancing Machine. I buy you a drink after your tour?" Rook asked.

"Got to take a rain check tonight, but nice you want to treat a lady right."

Lieutenant Esposito went back into the precinct with that fine ass of hers and Rook went to his vehicle. He called into the squad and left messages for both detectives that he was in town and working for

Phelps, on the Wayne Avenue double so they wouldn't get their panties in a bunch. Since the clock and the mileage were both running, he swung out to see Doc Nessel.

The Medical Examiner's Office was still in the same freestanding brick building with the three overhead doors in the back. Nessel's big caddy was in the parking lot. Lucas signed in, traded his Glock for a red plastic token, and handed the intake clerk his business card.

"I have an appointment," he said.

"Is he expecting you?" asked the sixty-ish woman with the beehive hairdo.

"I have an appointment now with Dr. Nessel." He looked at his watch.

Hairdo called back that there was a Mr. Rook to see him, pronouncing his name like the 'o's were from *zoo* or something. Then she asked if his first name was, "Lucas".

"It is. Just like the card says."

"Then Doctor Nessel will see you. He's with a patient right now, so it will be approximately one quarter of an hour."

"I'll wait," Rook told her, and he sat down to the offering of free neighborhood newspapers and a two year old copy of *Forensics*.

Twenty-five minutes later he went up to the front desk and asked Ms. Beehive that she check with the ME.

"He will summon you when he's available."

Lucas told the receptionist to tell Sam to "summon" somebody else and that he'd call him later. Then he went over to the intake desk and flipped them his token. "I'm out of here," he said.

The phone rang. It was Samuel Nessel, M.D. and he was ready for his visit.

Rook re-checked his weapon and went through the swinging doors and down the hall. The Medical Examiner was well under five feet tall, but didn't act like it, even when he knew people were looking at him like he was a circus freak. He came out from behind his desk as Lucas walked into the room.

"Welcome back to the City of Brotherly Love," he said, offering a stubby hand.

"Nice bow tie, Sam. When did you start that look?"

"When I mostly gave up smoking which is when they found that spot on my bladder. Lot of folks don't know about that risk, but the poison goes into your saliva, which means it's going to wind up in your urinary tract." He gestured for Rook to sit down. "Who can I do you for?"

"The name was Anna Lamb. Had a kid also DOA. Warren Phelps brought me in."

"Guests of mine. They belong to that cult in Mt. Airy." The Medical Examiner reached into his shirt pocket where he used to keep his cigarettes.

"The very same."

"You want to take a look? Got them on ice together although I'm not supposed to do that."

"What you got for me, Doc?"

"What I can tell you is what I told Detectives Moore and Lefkoe. Now there's a pair. The doer was left-handed and the efficiency of the cuts, I'm thinking he's done it before. Also, nobody did her, the other way, if you get my drift." the ME half-snorted a laugh.

Lucas stretched his leg. "You mean banged her?"

"No semen. Although he could have worn a condom and so on. Oh, and the decedent was breast feeding."

"You should be on one of them TV shows, Sam."

The dwarf adjusted his bow tie. "I'm waiting on Hair and Fibers, which is not my necessarily my field, and Tool Marks. Wounds, I know a lot about, particularly knife wounds, my father was *moel* after all.

"Which is what, Doc?"

"A rabbi who does the circumcision. A little joke here. By the way, I'm just fine in the equipment department."

"Terrific, I'm glad to hear that. You got anything for me on those knife wounds?"

The medical examiner took a note pad from his right desk drawer.

"Like I said, this will be in my written report and I already gave a verbal to Hawkey Moore and Lefkoe, the catching DT's, and Lieutenant Esposito, because Cisone's not around and she gives me a party in my pants. The knife wounds were the cause of death, the jugular veins and carotid arteries were severed on both the mother and the child. No stab wounds, no tissue bridging at all, so they were pure slice wounds.

"Tool Marks will have their say, but from where I sit, it's a fine, sharp blade, non-serrated, less than four inches, maybe a neck knife. You wear it around your neck," he gestured. "Something somebody with combat experience might have. No crime of passion here. Also, no cuts on the clothing or defensive wounds. Your doer just cut their throats, and like he's done it before. Pardon my use of the mother tongue again, but more like a *shochet* than a murderer."

"Which is?"

"In Kosher killing of the animal, one movement, one draw of the blade, that's it. Not that I'm saying that or putting it in my report. I'm just saying, no hesitation, no passion, a perfect cut, both times."

Rook wrote it down on the pad he took from the inside of his jacket.

"Plus the doer's a heartless fuck." He reached for the imaginary smokes again. "From what I see, she's nursing her infant when he cuts its throat."

"So the mother sees it, right? You telling me that Samuel?"

"Makes you sick," said the ME. "And I've seen plenty."

Rook got up. "Hug the missus, Sammy. I'm going to catch the fucker."

"Fuck him up, Lucas Rook. And I'm a physician talking here."

CHAPTER EIGHTEEN

Franklin Lamb fixed his special meal of lentil loaf as much to calm himself as for his family. After the evening meal and prayers, Brother Brodeur spoke to The Tau in their upstairs assembly room.

"Blessed be those who serve our One True Lamb of God."

They answered the same.

"Our Blind Messiah, Shoko Ashara, suffers in his imprisonment so that he may lead us again, *Ba-Abba*. Our Father will come, and we must serve him without reservations or hesitation. In times of good or of suffering. We do so by our prayers and acts of devotion. We are a family by his blessings. We are also our community in their community, so we shall act like one."

Brodeur walked to the window and back for effect and then embraced each one of the members of the Tau.

"The Last shall be First," said Brodeur.

The group answered him.

"And the First shall be Last," said their leader.

There were many things to do after their meeting, so Oleg Kutzenov retired to his office. The homicide detectives would be manageable. He had fooled many with his skills that far exceeded those of the Philadelphia Police Department. He dialed Northwest Detectives identified himself and asked for Detective Moore.

"Any other message?" asked Detective Radicchio.

"No, thank you," said Brodeur and he hung up.

After the Tau's family meeting, a number of the group came to his office with their problems or concerns. William Goodwin had tears in his eyes. His hands were balled into fists.

"You know who I am," he said. "You took me in." John Lamb began to weep. "I would never hurt our family. Anna, the baby…"

Brodeur got up from behind his desk. "Give freedom to your feelings, brother," he said. "Do not be ashamed. You are forgiven here. All is forgiven here, through the grace of our one True Lamb, Shoko Ashara. Kneel, John Lamb. Kneel in thanks."

William Goodwin knelt, and cried and cried, until he shook from it. Oleg Kutzenov let him go on despite the knocking at his door, so that others would know of the feelings and demeanor of John Lamb, who, if plans went well, would be so overcome by his guilt, that he would hang himself from the elm tree in the far right corner of their backyard.

The knocking at the door ceased and then began again in ten minutes.

"We are in prayer," said Brodeur. Then he turned again to William Goodwin. "You are to seek solitude this evening, John Lamb."

"I shall do as you have counseled me, Brother," said William Goodwin.

"May Our Lamb's blessings and comfort be upon you from His mind and heart of pure light," said Edmund Brodeur, as John Lamb left.

Victoria Lamb came to her spiritual leader's room shortly after. "I have brought you tea with buckwheat honey and fresh bread," she said.

"I'm fasting," he said. "For strength and guidance."

She nodded and left without speaking.

Oleg Kutzenov knew not to call the Philadelphia Police again. More than once, in itself was saying that you had something to hide. He had been interrogated by those much more skilled, and more vicious, but there was no need to be careless.

He reviewed the Tau's household expenses and then went over to the record store to resume the appearance of normalcy. Soon enough, he would meet with the detectives. And then, he would leave again to complete his assignment for the Foundation.

The unmarked police car pulled alongside of him on Emlen Street as he was leaving the store. Hawkey Moore slid his window down.

"Going somewhere?" he said.

"Do I know you?" Brodeur asked.

"Smart guy," said Gene Lefkoe. "Particularly you answering one question with another. You a smart guy?"

Brodeur started walking again.

Detective Moore gestured for Gene to cut him off and Lefkoe pulled up on the sidewalk.

Both detectives got out. "You trying to beat feet?" said Hawkey Moore.

A blue and white cruiser pulled up on the way to McDonalds for lunch "on the arm".

"Got this, girls," said Lefkoe.

"Don't go nowhere, Frenchy," said Lefkoe doing that dance of his.

"Of course," said Oleg Kutzenov. "But I don't know who you gentlemen are."

"Just returning your phone call is all. Now we can either have our little chat in my office right here or we can go down to Northwest Detectives."

"I prefer the latter, actually."

"What ladder?" said Gene.

"He means he wants to take a ride, partner. Maybe we take a detour along the way."

"I gather then, that you one of you is Detective Moore."

"You gather correct," said Hawkey. "Let's hear how you killed that mother and her baby. We get that on tape, how you were real-worked up about the baby's crying, like that, then we're done. Otherwise, we're going to lock you up and Jamaal and all his brothers are going to pound your ass forever for killing that infant."

"I didn't kill anybody. But if you persist with this completely inappropriate behavior, I am a clergyman after all, I shall call a lawyer."

Moore put his hand-tooled cowboy boot on the bumper of the Crown Vic.

"Can't hear a thing, pardner, can you?"

"Not a peep," said Lefkoe.

Detective Moore grabbed Brodeur and put him in the back of the vehicle, guiding his head so he couldn't claim police brutality. "We didn't even ask you any questions yet, so what do you need a lawyer for unless you did something real bad?" he said.

"I've done nothing," said Brodeur. "except tend to my congregation."

"You want to go back to your temple, is that it?" Lefkoe asked him.

"Our home."

Hawkey backed the unmarked off the curb. "Where everybody's got pretend names of 'Lamb', except you, that is."

"The Tau is a duly registered religious organization," said Brodeur.

"So they're like your flock or whatever."

"That is true, Detective."

"Then why's your DNA all over her? You some kind of pervert?"

Brodeur knew better.

"We do touch, hold hands in prayer, and I dispense blessings."

Hawkey Moore cut the wheel hard. "That's not all you dispensed to Anna Lamb," he said.

Oleg Kutzenov shook his head. "I have never touched her in that way. I never would."

"Markowitz, that's Anna Lamb's real name, right?"

"Correct," said Brodeur. "Her husband's name was Barry Ceisler from your perspective."

Moore cracked his window and took out a skinny cigar. "And you?" The detective lit his stick match with his thumb

"I'm just me."

"We'll see who's who, what's what," said Lefkoe.

"I don't understand," said Brodeur.

"You don't have to," Gene told him.

"Tell us about William Goodwin, Reverend."

"He's a member of our flock."

Hawkey Moore took a draw on his cheroot. "Who's been in jail for killing his own kid."

"I cannot discuss that."

"You don't have to," said Detective Lefkoe, as he stopped the Crown Vic in front of the Tau's property. "Don't go nowhere, like I said, Reverend," he said.

"Of course, not. There is much need here."

Oleg Kutzenov got out of the car and walked up the high steps. His anonymous call to the police to look at John Lamb had been successful. It had drawn their attention to William Goodwin as a prime suspect and would give them good reason to see his upcoming hanging as a suicide.

CHAPTER NINETEEN

Lucas Rook had wanted to keep his client on ice for a while. A loony-bird like that, he was likely to say anything, and anything other than, "I want my lawyer," would lead to "I killed my kid," not the best thing under the circumstances.

A surprise though, that Hawkey Moore and Lefkoe already grabbed your guy up for a little chitchat. They weren't Sherlock Holmes and Dr. Whoever. Most likely, somebody from the house or a neighbor called it in. Maybe Billy snored real loud or like that. Anyway, the best you can do is remind your client again that he's to give them only that Warren Phelps is his lawyer. Then you make another call to Moore and Lefkoe and head over to Broad and Champlost.

Rook was perfecting his art of sleeping with his eyes open in the waiting area when Sal Radicchio came over.

"What brings you down the turnpike?" asked Detective Radicchio.

"Babysitting, Sal."

"Anything to do with that double over on Wayne Avenue?"

"He lives with those fruitcakes, but he's not the type."

"This old timer is here with me," Sal told the desk sergeant. "Put in about 100 years in New York."

"He still got to sign in and show ID," said the desk. "Plus, he's coming in the House, he's got to secure his weapon if he's carrying and you've got to take him upstairs. Rules are rules."

"Sure they are. C'mon, New York. I'll hold your hand."

Rook did what he had to and they went up into the squad room. Computers had replaced the typewriters, but the desks were still World War II. Lieutenant Esposito was in her office, but she was on the phone.

"She put some junk in the trunk since you been here last, but she's still fine," said Radicchio.

"Cisone in?"

"Still out. Went to China or Korea or one of them gook places for a police convention. Me, I go far as Florida. You got me?"

"I got you, Sal."

Detectives Moore and Lefkoe came over.

"You selling girlscout cookies?" said Lefkoe.

"Just paying my respects. Working for Attorney Phelps. Babysitting John Lamb."

"He's right in the middle of this, up to his neck," said Hawkey.

"He's got squat to do with your double. And you both know that," Lucas answered.

"Right, right, New York. For nothing he's spending big coin for Warren Phelps?"

"Some things never change, boys. I just wanted to see your smiling faces."

"Keep your boy around," said Lefkoe.

"You want another chit chat, gents, give me or Warren Phelps a call. We'll be happy to give you what we got, which is squat."

"Don't let the door hit you on the way out," said Hawkey.

Rook drove back to the house with the hippies in it and had another face to face with Goodwin.

"You didn't give them just your name, Billy. Why did you do that?"

"I only told them about what happened at the rest stop."

"Which is what?"

"Somebody beat me up?"

"Which you told them why, Billy-boy?"

"Because I have rights."

"And because you're a dumb ass. You say anything else other than that?"

John Lamb kept quiet, which meant he did.

"And you told him that Warren represents you for what?"

"'For all things known and unknown, from the beginning to the end of time', like Judge Schwarzman made me memorize."

"That's swell, William. No more chitchat. You get the urge to say something or those detectives come back at you, you call me on my cel. I'm working 24/7."

William Goodwin was glad Lucas Rook was there. The remnants of the crime scene tape were still up, but the family had received permission to clean up the bloodstains.

Brodeur came down the steps.

"Brother Brodeur. He is our Guide and Pastor here," said William.

"We've met," Lucas answered."

"He took me in and saved me, Mr. Rook."

"As we have been saved," said Oleg Kutzenov.

Rook could smell the bad off of him, but said nothing.

"Perhaps you might stay for our evening meal and prayers, Mr. Rook," said Brodeur.

"I've got a previous engagement," Lucas said. "But like I've told William here, John whatever, if those two detectives come back or any other ones and I'm not here, he is to call his lawyer immediately." He took out one of his business cards and wrote Phelps' numbers on the back.

"But surely, the police will respect the sanctity of this temple."

"Just remember what I said. Meanwhile, I'm going to be parked out front for a while."

Brodeur went into the kitchen and then into the front room and out into the yard, checking on his flock. He set up a counseling session with Scott Lamb, and one for Victoria. Then he wrote on the community white board that he would be discussing a teaching of Shoko Ashara at evening prayer, which would be entitled, "Embracing Suffering," and went into his office.

There was still no contact from Reba Nemerov, which was either good or very bad. What Oleg

Kutzenov knew was that The Foundation's assignment must be completed quickly, lest he himself become one, particularly as there were the two policemen and the private detective nosing around. Fortunately, they were all as clumsy as the members of The Tau were sheep.

His strategy remained the same. All that was needed was John Lamb's suicide and a repeat or replacement of the fishing trip strategy, as The Foundation would direct.

Kutzenov checked the household assignments for that evening. After the meal and prayer, Victoria would do kitchen clean up and Franklin would check the furnace and the hot water heater. The evening meal was baked tofu and vegetables with soy ice cream as a distraction.

Brodeur was convincing in his presentation that suffering was part of The All and therefore should be received as the Messiah's blessing. Then lots of Father Cometh, *Ba-Abba*.

After, he gave his personal blessings and then went to his office, locked the door and checked his e-mail again. An ad for fishing off of Norfolk, Virginia appeared. "The Sweet Linda, Charter Availability." It came and went. His assignment had been repeated, the target reconfirmed.

There was lots of hemp in the Tau house. Just like the hippie children to become infatuated with the substance. A good clothing, and paper sources, and of course, there was the type which would make one intoxicated. While the Tau had strict rules against drugs and alcohol, there certainly was nothing prohibiting the utilitarian coil of rope kept in the tool shed. Soon William Goodwin would be hanging from it.

CHAPTER TWENTY

Detectives Moore and Lefkoe started their next shift at Northwest Detectives by checking to see if there was anything new on the board, not that their plate wasn't already filled with the mother and baby double on Wayne Avenue and the rest of their case load. The only thing posted was a reminder of the sensitivity training session.

"That training thing's obligatory, pardner," said Detective Moore. We got to go so that we can be reminded about being understanding to queers and not saying 'twat' or 'porch monkey' or the like."

"Porch-monkey twat," said Gene as he did his nervous little dance.

Detective Radicchio came up. "Saw your old friend from up the turnpike."

"Whoever could that be?" said Hawkey. "I don't have any friends north of Exit 7."

The training session was in an hour, just enough time to hit the Dunkin' Donuts and get back. Lieutenant Esposito came in. She had toned down her make-up.

"I appreciate those of you who had to bend your shifts and leave so we can get this all out of the way in one shot."

Somebody yelled something from the back. A lot of laughter and then some insults traded back and forth. Lieutenant Esposito let it go for about thirty seconds. "You got that out of your system? The sooner we do this, the sooner you can go back to being police."

Then she introduced Donna Houston from the Chief's Office, who talked for almost an hour about "Community Policing in the Increasingly Diversified Urban Center."

The lieutenant asked if there were any questions and then dismissed the group. Most of the detectives scattered, but Hawkey and Lefkoe hung around.

"Excellent presentation," said Moore, adjusting his string tie.

"Excellent job blowing smoke, Detective. Good try, though," said Esposito. "You want to get on my good side, you help Officer Mackrell transport his 'Occupy' street turd up to Friends Hospital. His unit's down. Piece of shit came down from New York."

"That's two of them," Lefkoe said, but Esposito let it be.

The uniforms brought the street person up.

"No farting, shitting or the like in our unit," said Detective Moore.

"My name is Robert Rhodi, with an "I"," he said, issuing a triumphant fart.

"You shit yourself, we're dropping you in the Delaware River," said Officer Mackrell.

Rhodi answered with another loud fart, followed by two shorter ones.

"Lovely," said Gene Lefkoe. "You play the trumpet."

Detective Radicchio walked Gene and Hawkey out to the parking lot in the rear while PO Mackrell brought his crazy.

"New one going up on the board, Sal," he said. "I appear to be up next, gents. One of those auto tag places, which is where I'm going. Guy buys his wife a pink caddy for their twenty-fifth. One of those older ones, but not a '59 or anything like that. The tag guy pockets the registration and sales tax so she can't drive the thing. The missus wants her vehicle on the road. Her hubby's got a '38 registered, she shoots Mr. Auto Tags right between the eyes."

"Got what he deserved," said Hawkey.

"That he did," said Radicchio. "You gentlemen interested in a decent meal, they just opened up an Indian place where Rodeo Ben's used to be."

"You playing me?" asked Lefkoe. "That's a joke, right? What do they serve buffalo or whatever?"

"Not that kind of 'Indian'," said his partner. "Like the dot head Indians. Anyways, we're on our way to our double. After we take Mackrell and his date to the prom."

"Maybe the shit stain and Rook can have a India sandwich."

"Fuck him," said Hawkey. "Jimmy Salerno hated his New York ass."

"Jimmy was good people, "said Lefkoe.

"Rook got the guy who got Jimmy," said Radicchio as he got to his unit.

"Fuck him any way," said Hawkey.

"Fuck him," said Gene.

They rode over to the nut-job hospital and then back across to the house on Wayne Avenue to see if their last visit had shaken anything from the half-assed minister or the baby killer pervert. Lucas Rook was parked out front. Moore put the bubble gum light up on the roof.

"You want some music to go with it, Gene?"

Lefkoe hit the siren and they pulled up right on Rook's Merc. Rook got out and walked toward them, "Philadelphia's finest," he said.

"You're moving pretty good with that bad leg and all," said Hawkey. "Plus, I heard you took three in the chest. What a little over a year ago?"

"What's on your mind here, ladies?"

"Ladies, my ass," said Lefkoe. "We're going to do our job."

"Knock yourself out, girls. You thinking about talking to my client, though, he's got Warren Phelps, which he already told you." He took out his cel.

"Don't you call inside or nothing, Rook," said Hawkey

"Just calling my client's expensive, ruthless, completely connected lawyer is all." He started back to his vehicle.

"You couldn't carry Jimmy Salerno's jock," said Lefkoe.

"Maybe you're right," said Lucas "But it was me who took out Delbert Fine in '05, and neither of you together are half of Salerno."

Rook called Warren Phelps, who called William Goodwin to say an associate from his office was on the way and not to say anything until he arrived. Phelps also called Northwest Detectives to remind them that he represented William Goodwin, now also known as John Lamb.

It took about five minutes for Hawkey Moore to get the reminder call not to question Goodwin without counsel present, which was okay because they just wanted to show up, stare at him, shake his tree and see what fell out. Nothing wrong with doing a little of the same with everybody else in the place. Plus some pressure on the so-called minister was certainly in order.

Edmund Brodeur had just put up the flyer for the rescheduled fishing trip when the two detectives came to the door.

Brodeur came over, "Would you gentlemen like some raspberry tea. It is very soothing for the nerves."

"Don't have any," said Hawkey adjusting the silver slide on today's bolo tie. "Thought we'd have another little talk though."

"Certainly, detectives," said Brodeur. "Our meeting room, or in my office?"

"Your office, "said Lefkoe. "We don't want to be spooking anybody."

Oleg Kutzenov smiled and took them upstairs. The room had a couch, two plain looking chairs and a wooden desk with a computer. There were no decorations, except pictures of Jesus and Shoko Ashara.

"Who's the Oriental?" asked Gene.

"I think the term you are looking for is 'Asian'. The other refers to rugs or furniture," said Brodeur.

"Right. What was I thinking?"

"The spiritual leader of our family, His Holiness, Shoko Ashara."

"Okay," said Hawkey. "And your little group here, who killed the lady and her baby?"

There was a knock on the door. Victoria Lamb with tea.

"May I let her in, Detectives?"

"Sure you can."

Victoria Lamb looked very good despite the plainness of her dress.

"You may put the tray down, "Brodeur said.

"*Ba-Abba*," she said.

He returned her greeting.

"And what language or whatever was that?"

"It's Hebrew," said Brodeur. "It means 'Our Father Commeth'." He waited for one of the two detectives to pick up their cup. When they didn't, he sipped his tea.

Moore and Lefkoe took turns with questions, background, and opinion, past, present and future.

Relevant and irrelevant. Polite and aggressive. After about forty-five minutes, there was another knock on the door. It was William Goodwin.

"I'm not supposed to speak to you, the police, but I have nothing to hide."

"You have the right to have your attorney present," said Detective Moore.

"And what if anything, you said to me, is privileged," said Brodeur.

"I did not hurt anyone. I did nothing."

"What kind of nothing did you do?"

Rook came through the door.

"Hey fellows," Lucas said. "I thought you understood he was represented. In fact, his counsel's about two minutes away."

Hawkey Moore got up. "His idea, not mine to have this little tea party. We didn't invite him. Maybe the Reverend here did."

Lucas walked over and took William Goodwin's arm. "You say zero without your attorney present, numb nuts."

"You're obstructing our investigation here," said Hawkey.

"Gentlemen," said the tall, red headed lawyer with the fancy brief case. "We're leaving. You wish to speak to our client, please make arrangements through Mr. Phelps." He handed each of them his card and followed Rook and Goodwin out of the room.

CHAPTER TWENTY-ONE

Hawkey Moore had Gene drive around the block a couple of times.

"Maybe we should call in New York's tag. We're lucky, we can tow that piece of shit sedan he's driving."

"Maybe we should," said Moore. "But we probably shouldn't."

"But we could do it anyways, Hawkey."

Lucas Rook came down the steep sets of stairs.

"Walks like an old man," said Detective Moore. "Holding onto the railing and whatnot. Jesus Christ."

Lucas came over to their unmarked.

Lefkoe slid the window down. "Can I help you?" he said.

"Looking for a lost dog."

"Meaning what?" said Hawkey.

"Take it anyway you want ladies, but you busting my stones like you've been doing's, not very friendly."

"We got police work to do," said Lefkoe.

"Was going to buy you girls a cold one or two, but my dance card's suddenly full."

"You get lucky and come-up with anything, Rook, you don't give it over, the best thing you're going to get is we see that license of yours gets pulled."

"Is that right, Detective Moore? I forgot about that, whatever it means, like you forgot I was wearing the gold shield when you were still in high school. So you have a nice day now." He turned and started over to his Mercury.

"You walk like an old man," said Lefkoe.

Lucas Room came back. "You want to step-out of your vehicle. Gene, Gene the Dancing Machine, I'll tune you up so even your partner here won't recognize you."

"The case is cleared, both of us got something for you," said Moore.

"Back to back, or two at a time, Hawkey."

Detective Moore gestured for Lefkoe to start up their unmarked and they swung away. Lucas went over to his Merc. The steps hadn't been easy with his leg the way it was and the extra weight he was carrying. He ever got his head right, he'd go on one of those diets Cat was always talking about. For sure though, he'd have kicked Lefkoe's ass and then Hawkey's.

The two of them together, he didn't know about, but wouldn't mind trying.

Rook drove down onto Lincoln Drive and took the Kelly into town. The road was named after the famous rower and his sister, Grace, the movie star. Word was the statue of him rowing was actually some other guy and that his sister was a whacko. Now they're famous forever, but still dead.

The Sheraton at 17th Street used to be The Franklin Plaza, but still gave a decent law enforcement discount. Shula's the steak place, wasn't there anymore.

He went up to his room and made some notes, including the "meeting" he just had with the two lunkheads. You don't write your time down, you're going to lose it. The couple of entries on the index cards he carried folded up in his wallet were good.

You generate maximum billing opportunities by working the case and shadowing William Goodwin, so Lucas called over to the ME to see if he wanted to meet, which no way the little fella was going to say 'no', the way he wanted to play cops and robbers.

"Nessel," the Medical Examiner answered his phone, like he was halfway a badass.

"Doc, Lucas Rook here. Thought you might want to grab a steak and beer. Talk about the case, old times, whatever." Lucas could hear him light a cigarette.

"Can't tonight, Lucas. I got family stuff to do. You know how that is." Which he didn't, unless you're talking about his twin brother, Kirk, who he got to watch bleed out into the gutter.

"Right, Sam. How's the wife?"

"Good, thanks for asking. Breakfast tomorrow would work. You know where the Melrose Diner is?"

"I'll find it."

"Eight, eight-thirty."

"Eight-thirty's good, Doc. See you tomorrow."

So it's grab something to eat downstairs or maybe at the Prime Rib later. Then, go back out and work Brodeur. And not just a little bit.

Neither Reba Nemerov nor Marat Belov were pleased with the meeting they had with their superiors at the Foundation. They were rebuked, given separate instructions and sent on their way.

Belov took the bus to New York City and then two cabs to meet with Teriyuki Mauritani. As he passed the doctor, he handed over a folded dollar bill. Then moved on.

Mauritani went to his room at the Marriott and examined the dollar bill by infrared light. What the "Earthquake Doctor" read chilled even him.

Reba Nemerov drove to Mystic, Connecticut where she enjoyed the nautical sights and then began her trip south. With her GPS disabled and avoiding EZ-Pass, only targeted surveillance would locate her. Nevertheless, she left the highways on more than one occasion and retraced her route lest she be followed or tracked. A mistake could mean the undoing of the Foundation's plan or her own death, which might be at the hands of Marat Belov, if that was what the Foundation directed.

Reba rested in her apartment that was two blocks from Northeastern University. Odd that someone with such a job and such a life should miss her cat, but she did. She was warmed as the black cat called Faustus, sat next to her on the recliner. Reba Nemerov sipped her herbal tea and whether it was that or the long drive, she drifted into sleep.

CHAPTER TWENTY-TWO

Rook was getting up when sawed-off Sam Nessel called.

"The wife got asked to be a fourth in this bridge game, a make-up game really. She's in this tournament…"

"Tournament, "Lucas said. "Is that a fact?"

"Right, right."

Lucas sat up and reached for his shoes with his feet. "Two no trump. Fore."

The ME lit up.

"Not good for your health, Sammy."

"Right. It'll stunt my growth."

"You got something for me on that double, Dr. Nessel?"

"Are you kidding? The way our budget's been cut we're still waiting on who shot President Lincoln. What I got is some theories, based on medical fact."

"And on your many years of experience?"

"Correct. Thank you. Maybe we talk about them over that steak and cold ones you were tempting me with."

"You thinking when, Doc?"

The ME took a long drag on his smoke.

"Sooner is better, Lucas. That way you can do what you got to."

"And you pick up Mrs. Nessel after she fleeces those, what you call them?"

"Bridge players. No, she drives. I'll pick you up or you can meet me at the Happy Rooster."

"Sansom Street, right. You still drive that big Cadillac?"

"Absolutely. I'll swing by in like half an hour."

"I'm good, Doc. I'll meet you."

"They know me there. They'll treat us right."

"That'll be peachy, Sam. Just peachy."

Nessel's going to give you something to work with or not. Probably not and he's just bored. Anyway, that's what expense accounts are for, so it's taking a good hot shower, even though its risking life and limb since there weren't those sticky things on the floor to keep you from slipping. Lucas stood under the hot water for a long time. Then, he dried off, put the same shirt back on, and went out for a cab.

The doorman's looking for a tip to pretend he made the cab materialize. You give him squat and take the second taxi.

Lucas got out at Walnut Street and walked over to Sansom and around the block. Then he went into the Happy Rooster to check it out before Nessel got there.

Sam comes waddling in and points to the bartender he's going to "his booth." The waitress, who looks like she has been doing a line or two, comes up and says she's sorry and then she gets the ME's Chivas and water, like she should have handed it to him the minute he came in. You're a dwarf, midget, whatever, you're going to have your usual spots where you spread some cash around so you get the celebrity treatment, and not that you're a freak.

The waitress brought his drink. Nice looking, mixed. "Hi Sam," she said.

"The usual for me, Deb."

She turned to Lucas. "The doctor is having our strip steak. I recommend it."

"Whatever the doctor's having," Rook said.

"Anything special for dessert?" said Nessel.

The waitress smiled, but it was one of those, I'm just working here, smiles.

The food he ordered was good and so was the second drink. What the Medical Examiner put out was good for nothing, though.

"And the killer," said Sam Nessel, "he's a pro because the wounds are so neat and clean, you could say, no hesitation, no passion. One, two, they're done." The Medical Examiner sipped his scotch. "Life's a bowl of shit soup. You said that once, Lucas."

"I was right then. I'm right now." And right that he already told you that stuff.

Nessel drank and then called over for another. It was clear the little get-together was to keep Sam company and nothing more. Rook picked up the tab, but let the ME run him back to The Sheraton.

The ME lit his second cigarette of the ride.

"Curbside justice, Lucas Rook. The fucker deserves it."

"Sure, Doc. Sure. Thanks for the advice. You okay I quote you in my report?"

"Not about that, what I just said."

"Sure, Doc. No way would I do that."

"My scientific impression, my medicine, absolutely."

The cab pulled up to the hotel. "Grab him up, Lucas."

Sammy sure liked cop talk.

"And put him down, Doc. I hear you."

Rook went up to his room and made enough notes to count as a "memorandum" to file. Then he wrote down his "preparation for meeting" and "meeting with the Medical Examiner." Together he had a little over three and a half hours, which was good use for the insurance money that pervert William Goodwin got from his wife dying.

Then he called Catherine Wren and told her everything was fine and he would be out to see her when he was done. Lucas changed his clothes so that he would be dressed appropriately for his surprise meeting with Mr. Brodeur. A black turtleneck and leather jacket and to complete his ensemble, his Glock .45 in the shoulder rig, and a back-up .38 to complete the fashion statement.

While Lucas got his Mercury from the Sheraton and rode out the Schuylkill Expressway to pay those religious creeps and maybe a killer, a serious visit, Franklin Lamb was going over the plans for the rescheduled fishing outing. Brodeur sat in the back of the meeting room in case there were any questions regarding the new itinerary and then led his small group in the first of the Tau's evening devotionals.

When Lucas Rook got to the hippies' place, the front door was locked and there was a sign posted that they were in prayer. This meant waiting in the vehicle for however long, which he had done a thousand times before.

So it's the old stakeout where you're lucky enough to have a partner, you're talking about getting laid or sports or the bullshit politics from One Police Plaza and at the same time, seeing who can hold their piss for the longest before one of you goes into the alley. You're by yourself, it's peeing on a tree or in some container you brought for that, which maybe they should give out in the Squad Room. You're working "so and so job" tonight, don't forget to vest-up and bring your piss bottle.

When the prayers were over, Brodeur announced that their fishing trip had been rescheduled for Virginia Beach for the coming Tuesday. "We shall go on with everything in this year of the so-called Apocalypse. It is the year 2012 and many of the unenlightened are frightened by foolishness. Evil is always possible, but Reality is our Messiah. *Ba-Abba.*"

"*Ba-Abba,*" answered his flock. And then Brodeur echoed, "Father is coming."

The Lambs went about their evening chores during which Oleg Kutzenov would stage the investigation-ending suicide of John Lamb. Something less complicated than the hanging for poor, despondent

William Goodwin because of all the comings and goings of the ridiculous policemen and that private investigator. They were marinating eggplant with Dijon mustard for tomorrow's dinner. The plastic bag would do just fine.

CHAPTER TWENTY-THREE

An hour and a half was plenty of time to sit in your vehicle, running up the bill. Lucas Rook started back up the three sets of steps to the Tau's house. There were those mushroom lights so at least he didn't have to go up all the way to see that the same stupid card was on the front door. Down the road were some fast-food places.

The burger joint gets graced by your presence to minimize the agro you're going to get being the only white face in the place if you hit the KFC. The parking lot is pretty filled up, but so is your bladder. So you park against the dumpster and get out, opening your jacket so you can have your Glock in your hand in a heartbeat. If that makes you a racist, you're a racist with a .45.

You go in the joint, hit the head, and are in line for your 3000 calories, when you can see on the manager's face that there's about to be a shitstorm of some sort. The girl with the headset who takes the orders, looks like she'd turn as white as a ghost if she could, which is telling you that there's stick up boys at the drive-through.

It is not a good idea to mess up a cop's mealtime, even if this one's not been a gold shield since before the fucknuts outside had their first wet dream. So you're out the front door and around to the line of cars, walking fast and low. The crime is about to go off, when Rook comes up on the Hyundai SUV, which has the bad guys in it.

You fire a round without justification's going to get you jammed up, and maybe your carry permit gets revoked. On the other hand, you don't get the stick-up boys' attention fast, they're just as likely to put a couple of holes in the girl.

The sound of your Glock exploding the left front tire is enough to get the scum bucket's attention.

"Drop it fellows. You don't, I'm making you both cripples for life."

The driver complies. His running buddy doesn't. You shoot him, gets you in way jammed-up. So you use one of your many street smarts, which is to put a round in the dashboard. The sound is deafening, which gets bad boy number two to drop his weapon and his bowels, judging by the smell of things.

"I count to three, you fellas still here, I'm going to cap both of your black asses. One…"

The closest one turned to look at Lucas. "Where your badge if you 5-0?"

Rook pushed his automatic in the scummer's ear. "You don't want to get dead, drop your weapons out the window and roll, blown tire and all."

Even though Wayne and Chelten was a main intersection and shots were fired, Rook was back at the Tau spot by the time the patrol car from the District arrived. The "At Prayer" sign was still on the Wayne Avenue door. Fuck it. Tomorrow was another day.

Lucas Room went back down to his room at the Sheraton, stopping on the way for a couple of slices of pizza and a six-pack. A lovely evening watching cable and getting heartburn. Catherine Wren called on his cel that she misses you which you tell her "me, too" and sack out.

Bright and early, the next morning, the room phone rings. It's the esteemed Samuel Nessel, MD. "You told me you were staying at the Sheraton. I called around," said the Medical Examiner.

"Great spadework, Sam. Or am I not allowed to say that?"

"Sure, Rook. I get it. Sure. I got something for you."

Lucas sat down and took out his note pad and the pen from the dresser. "Shoot," he said.

"I got a hold of the Tool Marks report. You want the long version or what I call the, "the other version."

"Whatever makes you happy, Doctor."

"So from the medico-legal perspective, microscopic examinations look for individual, class and sub characteristics to conclude the type of tool. Here it seemed obvious to me we were dealing with a knife wound, a KCW, we call it "knife cut wound, not KSW, which would not be relevant here, because there's no stabbing. The wound was almost like a pencil line."

"Okay," said Lucas.

"Right. I guess I'm going on and on. So what I've got is the report puts the thickness of the blade at .40 mm, which makes it a surgical blade. You know, like a scalpel. That doesn't necessarily mean it's a doc though. Could be a hobbyist you know, somebody who does carvings, boats, model airplanes."

"Which is why, Sam?"

"Micro particles of wood. We're waiting for a final draft, but cedar is the preliminary classification. I thought that might mean something to you."

Lucas Rook got up and put his shoulder rig back on and strapped his back-up to his ankle. "Appreciate it, Dr. Nessel. I'll get back to you tomorrow. We'll have a couple of pops, put the feedbag on. My dime."

He went back out to his Mercury and called Hawkey Moore, but couldn't get him. Lefkoe wasn't in either. Rook finally got Esposito.

"Lieutenant, where's the Gold Dust Twins? I got something for them."

"Moore's RDO. Gene's at the podiatrist. Gene, Gene, The Dancing Machine at the foot doctor, quite a coincidence."

"Right, right. You want to call the cowboy on his cel at home, tell him I got the clearance on his double, which I'm going to hand him if he gets out of his easy chair."

Reba Nemerov rang the bell at the Tau's house as Rook was starting on his way there.

"Can I help you?" said Phyllis Lamb.

"Monsieur Brodeur," she said.

"I shall see if he is available. Do you have an appointment?"

"I am his sister," Nemerov said.

"I'm sorry. Please do come in."

Oleg Kutzenov had no sister, but he hid that with skill equal to his anger and concern, that his likely visitor had either broken protocol to deliver something of great importance or was there to kill him. He put his subcompact automatic in its wallet holster and went down to see her.

"Brother," she greeted him with a kiss on the cheek.

"So glad to see you. Is mother well?"

"May we sit down and have a cup of coffee? It has been a long ride," she said.

"Yes, yes. Let's go back into the kitchen."

They went down the hall. Both were silent until they had closed the door behind them.

"You should not have come here," said Oleg Kutzenov.

"Perhaps you are right, brother," said Nemerov as she shot him. Kutzenov ducked and turned at her first movement so the round took off his ear and a sliver of his skull. He went down bleeding profusely, trying to staunch the flow with his hand as he rolled across the floor for safety.

"You look silly, brother," said Reba. "Like some wiggly worm." She stood over him. "You made some people very angry with what you did here. And plans had to be changed. That's the worst thing, you know. Perhaps there is your wonderful ice hockey in heaven."

She put the next two rounds into him. The "pop-pop" from the silencer was hardly noticeable outside the room.

Oleg Kutzenov fired from his pocket as she delivered her coup de grace. One of his shots struck her between the legs. The other blew out her femoral artery. The two of them died as Lucas Room pulled up to the house on Wayne Avenue

Rook went up to William Goodwin's room, then shoved him against the wall, and snatched the cross from around his neck. "What have we here, Billy Boy?" he said. But he came up with nothing.

Victoria Lamb came running out of the kitchen. Her hands were covered in blood. "They're both dead," she said. "Brother Brodeur and a woman."

"Don't go anywhere," said Lucas Rook as he dragged Goodwin down the steps, and then quickly tied his hands and feet with plastic restraints.

Rook went to look at the bodies. "Nobody touch anything, and nobody move."

"You got a mess here," said Detective Moore as he entered the room.

Scott Lamb started to speak, but Hawkey shut him up. "Add that to your list, people. Nobody says anything neither until you're asked."

Two cruisers pulled up and secured the scene. Then Gene Lefkoe came in. "What did I miss?" he asked.

"Give me what you got, Rook," said Detective Moore.

"That's why I called you, cowboy," Lucas said.

They went into the hall where they could watch John Lamb, and what was going on in the kitchen.

"Everybody go into your rooms until somebody comes to get you," said Detective Lefkoe.

"So New York, tell me what you got?" said Moore.

Lucas took the wooden symbol on the leather cord from his shirt pocked. "Figure this is the murder weapon. Slit your two vics' throats."

"How'd you figure that?" said Lefkoe.

"Tool Marks report, which I haven't seen, says it's a real thin blade, got bits of cedar on it, so I figure it's in this cross, like some Chinese puzzle."

"You take from which of these folks?"

"The baby killer I got tied up over there. Do it once, you'll do it again. I checked his, but it didn't open or whatever."

"I like it," said Moore. "Then again, we got them bodies in the other room."

"Which no way is not related somehow," said Lucas.

The two Philly detectives and Rook went into the kitchen while Officer Mackrell took care of William Goodwin.

"The chick, good looking. Hell of a thing to do her crotch that way."

"Terrible waste, partner," said Gene. "Terrible"

"You're getting the clearance on the double, you can do the honors in here," said Lucas Rook.

Detective Moore removed the Tau from around Brodeur's neck. It slid open to show the stainless blade. "I'll be damned," he said.

"Been there," said Rook. "Now whenever you two heroes want my statement, I'll be happy to oblige."

CHAPTER TWENTY-FOUR

Lucas Rook jotted down what he had and checked out of his room. He waited until he was halfway back up the New Jersey Turnpike before he called The Swan. First at the office where the service said they'd try and reach Judge Schwarzman and then on his cel.

"Sorry to disturb you, Judge, but I wanted a face to face before I meet with the Philly PD."

"About my client, I assume."

"Correct."

"Where are you now?" asked Schwarzman.

"About Exit 9."

"Small world. Our mutual lady friend is taking me out for pizza."

Rook swung around a slow moving minivan.

"Trenton, I'm guessing," said Lucas. "I could come to your office tomorrow early. Or I could call Warren Phelps, Whatever you want."

"We could meet at whatever this place is called."

"La Penta's" said Grace.

"That'll work." Lucas took the next exit and headed back south. Good old-fashioned 4-1-1 and asking directions got him here. You get one eye on your GPS, you only got one on the sixteen wheeler that's about to run you off the road.

The place was jammed, but Carrington got out of the Swan's limo and got a tomato pie and a pizza with everything that was going to stink-up the vehicle for a week. He didn't have word one for Lucas, which was fine all the way around, until Gracie started up that they should "shake on it" because they were "trail buddies."

Jake Schwarzman took a couple of slices and got into Rook's Mercury where he heard about what had happened down in Philly.

"They question my client, Lucas?"

"They're not looking at him, Judge. Plus, me and the lawyer from Phelps' got it on the record that he's represented."

The Swan nodded a thankyou and finished his mouthful. "They know about his history."

"They don't care. I just cleared their double for them, and they got another two for good luck."

"He do anything he shouldn't have other than find himself at a murder scene?"

"Got pushed around by a handsome devil, who he'll probably want to sue."

Schwarzman wiped the grease off his fingers and rolled up the paper napkin. "I'll take care of that. I'll get to Warren so both you and Goodwin have counsel down there if you need representation."

"Anything you want me to say or not, Judge?"

"Let's wait for your report and until I've spoken to Warren."

Grace Savoy came over and knocked on the window.

"Boy, "Do I have news for you, cowboy?" she said.

"Which one?" asked Schwarzman.

"The one who is not my sugar bear."

"Lawrence was so moved that in D.C. you did not break his face and that my nipples stood erect like those English soldiers guarding the Queen, that I'm going to some island, a vacation spot, to shoot a big money layout for a 'retrospective'. That's going to mean Jake and I will be vacationing for a few days. You can meet us there."

Rook looked at the Swan. "You two enjoy yourselves."

"Lawrence said you should be there, too, neighbor man," said Grace Savoy. "It'll be good money."

"We'll talk about it," said Lucas.

The judge reached into his million-dollar suit and took out a fancy cigar. "For your friend with the garage."

"He'll appreciate it."

"E-mail Phelps your interim bill, Lucas. Send me a blind copy, first thing."

"Appreciate it, Judge."

"And don't forget the mileage."

Rook headed North, hoping to catch Catherine at home in Princeton, but she was in the City taking care of her father.

She started to cry, when Lucas got her on the phone.

"I'm on my way," he told her.

What Rook knew he could do for Cat and her old man was not much of anything except keep her company, which she seemed to need. There was a nurse there and a doc came over. The old guy made it through the night, which the lady in white said was a good sign.

When the medical things calmed down, Rook went over to his place, coffeed up, showered, and put on one of Muskrat's discount shirts, and headed back to Philly to rack up some more billing and maybe think about that trip.

The boat ride from Morocco to the Canary Islands, "Island of the Dogs," would have been pleasant if the single man traveling with a single bag were a different kind of person. Similarly, the natural beauty of the Isla de la Palma with its panoramic view and miles of cobblestone paved hiking trails, would have been a delight to someone else.

This traveler had other things on his mind. Marat Belov waited until the ocean's fog shrouded his brief ascent and then deposited his suitcase into one of the openings in the Cumbre Vieja volcano. "Vents," Dr. Mauritani said they were called.

When he was safely away, Belov would detonate the twenty-five pound suitcase nuke he had bought from Osama Bin Laden's more enterprising survivors at the original purchase of seventy million dollars, plus ten percent. From the Russian stockpile to the black market to a pushy Islamist now dead, into the hands of a Russian servant of Shoko Ashara.

A pity that The Blind Messiah would not see the thousand foot high wave rushing at the speed of a jet plane across the Atlantic to obliterate Washington, D.C.

"*Ba-Abba*," said Marat Belov, though no one in the small plane heading in the opposite direction would understand him. "Father is coming."

END